Ishtar Coming Part II

Ishtar Coming

Mahir Salih

Published by Mahir Salih, 2024.

ISHTAR COMING PART II

First edition. May 8, 2024.

Copyright © 2024 Mahir Salih.

ISBN: 978-1399975827

Written by Mahir Salih.

Chapter One

Baghdad to Dubai — Spring 2007

The dented Iraqi Airways plane was preparing to touchdown on the tarmac at Dubai International Airport. An air hostess announced its arrival to the unofficial capital of the United Arab Emirates. The passengers had lost their patience despite the short journey of only two and a half hours. Selma sat comfortably in her economy-class seat, ruminating about the good old days when she used to fly freely to Europe and the United States in the 1970s. Years when the Iraqis enjoyed oil-boom rewards, and snapped up bargains from London shopping centres, mainly Oxford Street, in the summer and then headed to Kuwait in winter. These were shopping journeys in the free-capital market of the West because they could not find the variety or the quality in State-controlled trade in Iraq. Now, that was history. Selma was not familiar with the name Dubai back then. Dubai signifies the word *glamour* and *elegance* with only two words.

She woke from her daydreaming when the pretty air hostess, wearing her green-silk dress, which matched with her colour-coordinated cotton hat, tapped her gently on the shoulder.

'Madam, we are about to arrive.'

Selma opened her eyes after her nap. She felt a tremor in her limbs. *What is next?* she wondered.

She had just re-lived the civil war in Iraq, which she had left behind her, with flashbacks. Horrors of war, which she could not forget, would traumatise her forever. The war raged after Saddam Hussein had been deposed, and the vacuum created by the Allied Forces could never be filled. Pro-Iran military militia reciprocated equally as ruthlessly as Sunni forces funded by the West and the Gulf State to counteract the Shia expansion in a triangle that consisted of Iran, Iraq and Syria. Images of blood and dead bodies and restless nights had followed her,

1

but she was comforted by coming to an unknown new land where she believed the footpaths were paved with gold.

She grabbed her fake Dolce and Gabbana brown crocodile handbag sent to her by her son, Ahmed, who was by then well established in UAE. It was one of the only precious possessions that she managed to get out of Iraq along with a few golden earrings and rings hidden inside her bra. This would stop her valuables being detected at the chaotic Baghdad Airport, especially when she pretended to be an elderly helpless woman. She glanced at her diamond wedding ring and recalled how she had lost her husband. Hassan, who was almost killed in the cross-fire between American troops and the insurgents or terrorists as each side called them. Yet alcohol had the final say in finishing him off. She was left alone and penniless after her daughter joined her Aunt Zelfa and travelled to the United States with the US refugee scheme that arranged the transfer of Iraqis who had collaborated with the United States forces.

Hardship, war and the international embargo all combined and helped to make Selma penniless. She lived off handouts from relatives until her son settled in Dubai with a good job in the commercial port. He received sufficient pay to support himself and his widowed mother.

Life took a positive turn when her son invited her to live with him. It was her only way out of poverty and destitution. It was to be her new lease on life to regain some of her faded social status.

She lifted her plump, curvaceous body with difficulty from the space where she had squeezed into the small aeroplane seat. She thought about how much weight she had gained as she approached her late sixties. She walked with difficulty, and struggled in her cheap, locally-made, high-heeled shoes. She was expecting that the heel could break at any minute, but she begged them not to fail her. The shoes were made by a local industry that relied on available resources for what was now called up-cycling and the only way to cope with an austere means of living.

The air hostess guided her to the toilet with a polite warning to hurry as landing was imminent. She shut the toilet door with difficulty and locked it. When she looked in the mirror, she gave a shout of extreme horror. *What a frightening look, where did those wrinkles come from?* She could not believe the youthful, beautiful woman she used to be and how she was now. The hard years, full of stress, had added extra years to her age. She used Botox in Baghdad, that had smoothed the deep lines around her eyes and her mouth but not enough to regain her prime looks. She applied a new layer of Rimmel foundation, in a desperate attempt to fill the wrinkles before she coated her lips with fresh lipstick. She saved the Rimmel brand for special occasions. She didn't care about its expiry date.

Selma tried to adjust her head covering. She felt suffocated with the *hijab*, she had to wear after the fall of Saddam Hussein which was followed by chaos with the lack of security and the deliberate dismantling of the security protocol that controlled law and order with a firm hand.

She remembered with pain when she was prevented from filling her car with fuel at a petrol station. A male teenage militia had ushered her aside, and much to her shock had prevented her having access to petrol.

'You are not allowed to fuel your car because your bare head is against Islamic regulations,' he said.

Her thoughts were interrupted by the hostess knocking on the door.

'Please get ready; we will land soon.'

Selma examined her face and muttered. 'Never give up. The modern world has changed everything. Plastic surgery is the way forward. Many of my friends have had liposuction to remove fat and dermal filler to fill wrinkles.' At that moment she recalled the days of murder in the streets and the chaos after the US troops occupied the streets of Baghdad. But it had not deterred desperate women from fixing what years of suffering had caused. She tried to adjust her head covering and contemplated her features without it. She took it off. 'I cannot wait to get rid of it,' she said to herself.

With a struggle, she opened the toilet door to face the pretty well-made up face of the air hostess who had a concerned expression on her face. It was difficult to hide under the thick layer of make-up. She tried to hold Selma's hand to guide her to the seat.

'Don't you dare touch me,' said Selma. The poor girl almost lost her balance and was shocked at Selma's rude and disparaging remark. She tried to be indifferent, so she didn't hurt the old woman's feelings. She was only trying to help.

I am not old. If anything, the hostess is not much younger than me.

Selma trotted slowly but steadily to maintain her balance on her cheap high heels. It was a constant worry that the shoes would betray her and break. She fell into her seat and made an impressive amount of movement against the passenger next to her as she tried to fasten her seat belt with difficulty. She realised the pounds she had piled on during the days of war, when she'd been besieged and hampered by restricted movement, plus the protein diet that she could hardly afford. She went from denial to reality. After a few failed attempts, she managed to fasten the belt. Yet again she reminisced about the good days when she used to travel in the 1970s. What a different experience that had been. She had struggled to overcome her fear and anxiety to board a plane. Something she had missed when Iraq went through endless years of war and travel prohibition.

Selma felt the vibration through her old body when the plane's wheels touched the tarmac. She released a sigh of relief in the safety of her new home, even though she hadn't had a choice.

The loudspeakers deafened her ears with the landing announcement in English and Arabic.

Selma felt her heart pounding like a machine. *What if Ahmed is not at the airport? Where will I go and what will I do? Is this the right decision?* Questions bombarded her head. But what could she do? She had no one else to live with in Baghdad and was without resources with which to survive. After the mass migration from Iraq, her children had left home. She could not cope with her older, strict, spinster sister, living under the same roof. Thus, she had accepted her eldest and only son's invitation to live with him in his newly adopted country. Nevertheless, he was not doing her a favour. It was the duty of the eldest son to look after his ageing parents; to follow the cultural tradition.

The plane settled smoothly on the tarmac. Selma opened the curtain and was struck with the golden rays of June sun. Her son had warned her about the heat and humidity in the summer. She was perplexed by his comments when he said Baghdad weather was refreshing in July. Had he forgotten the heat in Iraq?

'You will be surprised how much hotter it is in the United Arab Emirates, Mother,' he said to her astonishment.

Selma shuffled her way through the endless and vast Dubai Airport corridors, trying to read the Arabic directions to customs. She was welcomed by a stern face of the woman customs' official who asked her the purpose of her visit. Selma was in fear of being deported back to Iraq and she answered with a shaky voice. 'I'm joining my son.'

The young Emirates' girl smiled broadly. She had enhanced lips, a pretty face and her hair covering matched her suit. The woman stamped her passport and welcomed her in Arabic.

Joining her son was going to be magic. Her son had given her strict instructions about what she had to do and where to go, but all of it had evaporated from her head. Now she was in a panic. Selma rushed towards an Asian male worker. He spoke to her in broken Arabic and pidgin English.

'You need help madam?'

'Yes, I need to collect my suitcases.'

'Which flight you came on?'

'The one from Baghdad.'

'Please follow me.' He guided her to the carousel to collect her three huge suitcases loaded with all the goodies to please her son after a long separation. The young man carried the luggage on a trolley, and she followed him obediently to the passengers' exit. She was puzzled and excited as she searched for her son who she had not seen for five years. She wondered if he had changed or aged or even looked younger because he had less hardship. She dismissed the latter that could indicate her looking so much older.

Amid the passengers and their loved ones waiting for them, and all the noise, she heard a familiar voice, which was followed by a strong hand that touched her shoulder. She turned to see Ahmed, with his prematurely grey hair. He was in his late thirties and there were grey circles around his eyes caused by his sleepless nights at work.

'*Alhamdulillah ala al salama,*' Ahmed greeted her with kisses, and thanked God for her safety.

'My sweet boy. You are all I have got now. I have lost everything,' she said as they hugged each other dearly. To the astonishment of everyone around them, they groaned, and cleared their throats of excitement and pain.

He carried her luggage on the trolley and pushed it towards the car park.

'I have bought a second-hand car,' he said with immense pride knowing it would be difficult to impress a difficult woman, who mocked anything and everything.

She examined the car with her green eyes. 'Not too bad,' she said.

Chapter Two

After The Fall of Baghdad

The sun was too warm for late June in 2007. The streets were quieter than usual after sunset. The inhabitants of Baghdad had a habit of going to the Tigris River to inhale the cool refreshing spring wind that passed by the eternal river. Nevertheless, the regular Baghdad River frequenters missed the fun of the cafes and restaurants that had been built in the Gryat district on the outskirts of Al-Adamiyah to replace the once sought after Abu Noas Street which lost its glamour in the 1990s and was now only frequented by men seeking masgouf fish or men getting drunk on the local *arak* spirt while they were in the company of prostitutes or with their friends.

The smell of the grilled faloja kebab went in vain. There were no customers to eat or be greeted by the few scared male waiters, who lived in fear of their safety. Some adventurous citizens dared to grab a quick bite of a kebab sandwich wrapped with local *samoon* bread that contained salad or pickles as they fled stray bullets from unknown sources.

Baghdad had become a no man's land war zone since the country fell apart because there was no security or body to govern it. The Americans had no plans or ideas about how to run the country. They lacked the experience to manage a country that had been run with an iron fist for over thirty years during Saddam Hussein's reign. The military militia affiliated to different sects, served certain powers and were in conflict as they tried to take over each other and ultimately the country, all the while serving their masters' interests in the region. The sight of innocent dead victims lying in the streets was a common one in what had once upon a time been one of the safest countries.

The population of Baghdad had hidden inside their houses, in anticipation of a shower of bullets or even bombs from either the insurgents, terrorists or US soldiers. There was no discrimination at any time of the day or the night.

At the centre of Adamiyah and Al Sabah Streets, a huge mansion suffered as it was battered by war either directly from bombing or from lack of maintenance because of the cash shortage — old money was not enough to meet its needs.

In a mansion built in the 1930s, in a street adjacent to Al Sabah Street, Loma was squeezed with her old maid in a box room. They were crunched together as they listened to a radio recital of verses from the Quran. She hoped to protect herself and her children from imminent danger and avoid indiscriminate shelling. Amid the chaos that had taken place, her husband, Riaz, was on the run, having been targeted by the new order militant forces who were headhunting the old regime's symbols. Riaz had become one the most prominent members of the Ba'ath Party in previous years. He had received the highest accolade from Saddam Hussein with all the privileges included from the previous era. Now he was high on the wanted list. And had been labelled as a public enemy, not far behind the number one, Saddam Hussein.

It had been over ten years since Loma had left him to seek a life of freedom and independence she had always longed for. He had declined to agree to a divorce. He could not go through this process and save face from humiliation and rejection by society, and the status as a divorcee would bring him down in political circles. He would be told, *If you could not handle your wife, how could you handle a country.* Loma and Riaz agreed to have an amicable separation.

But much to her dislike, in public they pretended to be together on the condition that she had custody of her boys. In reality, she and Riaz lived separate lives. As part of their agreement, they were obliged to attend social functions, presidential and government official engagements together. Loma thought of it a small price to pay to be with her children. She realised that she would have to keep up the pretense, at least in public, to keep custody of her children.

Riaz did not waste time benefiting from his freedom. Immediately, he began dating other women from actresses, singers and socialites to gypsy prostitutes while Loma devoted her life to her children and her mother who had succumbed to old age before the turbulent events that took place in the country.

In times of distress, she lived on memories of her lover, Ali, who had received death threats from Riaz's cronies and had to leave the country in haste. He felt lucky that his head was still attached to his body since the toppling of the old regime. She had nothing left but her two precious gems — her two boys.

The boys grew up rapidly and finished university and secured lucrative jobs with the aid of their father's and the political party influence. Her boys got married and Loma became a grandmother with three grandchildren. It was a mother's duty to secure the bloodline of the future family and to ensure her offspring completed her mission in life in accordance with tradition. The irony was, after all the planning and arrangements, her sons were on the run with their father, and she heard nothing of their whereabouts. They too were headhunted, having been affiliated to the last remaining symbols of the old regime.

Loma left her lavish mansion at al-Mansur in the posh district of Baghdad and took refuge at her mother's modest one in al-Adamiyah. It was a safer option, but equally dangerous to live next door to her forever enemy Selma. The latter had left her with endless nightmares when she popped into her mother's house to welcome Loma.

'So, you are on the run,' she said. Her tone was sarcastic and triumphant after Loma returned from the UK.

'No one is safe, Selma.' She recalled the conversation that took place with Loma during the first week as she settled down at her mother's house after the riots took place following the US led invasion of Iraq.

'Not to worry. I am on your side. My husband has misled the fighters looking for your husband. We have been friends for such a long time, after all.' Loma could not utter a word that might upset Selma, or else she and her family would end up with an unknown or perhaps well-known fate.

The positive side to the disappearance of her boys and her husband meant that they were immune to any slander from Selma, or anyone like her. And there was no shortage of these people under such circumstances.

Loma was hopeful that Selma would not cause havoc, because of her secular way of life and thinking. Her way of being was not a good idea given the new chaotic and fanatical order. She had no affiliation with the extreme religious principles imposed on the masses by extremist groups. She dismissed her thoughts, yet she could not ignore the noise of shooting or the stray bullets coming from amateur teenagers lured and brainwashed to become the bitch of opportunistic, power-thirsty warlords who were keen to have a big slice of the pie.

Loma was mesmerised by the old landline handset as she waited for a phone call from her nearest and dearest to hear the latest news. The lines had been cut off after the relentless bombardment of the Allied Air Force against the ailing Iraqi infrastructure, which had been battered for over a decade by western embargo, following the invasion of Saddam Hussein to Kuwait. She could not talk to the rest of her family and friends and was dying to know the fate of her children and grandchildren. She had no access to a mobile phone, which were only available to the old regime VIPs and intelligence sector but not to the general public.

She spent her days buying the necessary groceries from local shops, avoiding long-distance journeys and only going out before sunset. She also avoided revealing her real identity by disguising her voice and not responding to phone calls or answering the door. She was confronted once by Selma in a public place while she was queuing for a gas cylinder that she needed to cook her simple meals of vegetable stew and rice and to provide her with warmth in the winter.

'I bet you are surprised to wait for that long to get some of the basics we have always taken for granted.' Such inflammatory statements could mean she risked her life, and she could not afford to do that. Slandering was a common occurrence in such a paranoid atmosphere. But the consequences were dire.

She remained in sheer fear of Selma's revenge since Loma had orchestrated her imprisonment where she had endured a bitter experience that she had endured until a presidential pardon came from Saddam Hussein on his birthday. She was one of the lucky ones.

Rumour had it that her husband, Riaz, had fled the country, but to where? That was anybody's guess. She'd heard fleeting, unfounded stories about the fate of others who she knew had affiliations with the old regime. Her old flame Bilal was one of them. She wept bitterly when she learnt Bilal had been murdered while defending his masters.

'What a waste,' she said when she learnt about his futile fate from her gossipy neighbour, Soad, who was a potential menace to her safety if her gossip and loose tongue were combined with Selma's vindictive plans.

Al-Adamiyah could have been a safe haven for its Muslim Sunni population despite their dislike of the ancient Saddam Hussein regime, including its symbols such as Loma, who continued to associate with his ex-regime, after having shared the same Muslim Sunni sect with the Islamic fighting group in a raging bloody civil war centred in Baghdad.

The city had changed. There were no bars, restaurants or night clubs open; they used to be open twenty-four-seven.

Loma had forgotten the grief she suffered when her mother died. She could not conduct a proper funeral burial under the showers of bullets and shells that targeted mourners who came to bury their loved ones in the cemeteries and to identify with their religious affiliations.

Even though she was full of thoughts about past events, including the very recent ones, she was still wise to the bitter reality. When the phone rang, it sounded too harsh because she was anxious about receiving unhappy news as was the norm under such circumstances. A faint voice spoke. It was unclear.

'Loma, it's me,' said the voice.

The handset fell from her hand. She gave a cry of surprise. After composing herself and trying to form words with a dry mouth, she realised that she should not mention names in case the lines were censored as they used to be during Saddam Hussein's era, despite the state of chaos and lack of censorship. It had come about as a result of the outcome of the dismantling of all the security infrastructure. She was aware that all Saddam's tactics had fallen apart and there was no government in control. All that remained was fear. It was then that she realised the voice was her baby son, Raad.

'Yes, I know. How are you and where are you?' she replied.

'My brother and me have reached United Arab Emirates.'

Loma gave a sigh of relief which was followed by a period of silence. That was all she wanted. She did not have the energy or the will to ask about his father's fate. *Who cares!*

'And your children? Loma asked in a gentle whisper in anticipation of hearing bad news.

'We are all fine.' The short pause seemed ages to Loma. 'Mother, I want you to join us,' he added.

'Why, dear? I cannot renew my passport,' she replied in a helpless tone.

'Do not worry. I have arranged it with someone. I have paid a hefty bribe.'

'Then it is possible?' she said and uttered a sigh of relief. 'How is your brother?'

'He is fine. He lives in al-Sharjah close to Dubai. I'll talk to you later, but please come.'

'I will, I will; for sure, but I want to speak to my baby boy,' she said with a big sigh of concern. At that moment, he disappeared from the line. She had nothing in her life to look forward to but her children. Before she could collect her thoughts and take in the huge turn of events, the doorbell pierced her ear drums. She rushed to her small shelter to hide from fear of the unknown, uncertain what could possibly come next. Who could be calling at this time? The bell sound changed to knocking and she heard a soft familiar voice. She moved from her crouching position on the floor and shuffled her body, which was luckily still slim enough to fit her tight trousers that she'd worn ten years ago. The soft voice became clearer as she approached the door.

'It is Soad; open the door, Loma. It's me Soad; do not worry.'

All of a sudden, Loma gained the confidence to stand upright, although she was unable to walk on her shaky legs. 'What do you want?' she asked with sudden and unexpected courage.

'Please open the door; it is urgent.'

Loma thought what else could it be? If death awaited her, then it was a mercy. She opened the door with hesitation and curiosity.

'How do you know my whereabouts?' Loma's tone was aggressive. She had a need to protect herself.

'Everyone in al-Adamiyah knows you are at your mother's place.' Her words were uttered with confidence to cover his humiliation and undermine Loma's stance. 'That's why I am here to warn you,' she added.

'Warn me about what?' Loma asked.

'You know your connection with Saddam Hussein's regime is well known around here.'

'But everyone knows that I am separated from my husband.'

'Are you? That's not the way it looks. You are driving a lavish Mercedes car and buying clothes from Europe. People are in an extreme rage about the previous regime and link you to it.'

'What should I do?' Loma dropped her aggression and became a submissive victim, like a sheep waiting its turn in the abattoir.

'Listen, people are fleeing like Selma did. You are lucky that she has fled to somewhere good. I'm sure she would have reported you to the Americans or even worse to the Shia affiliated fighters.'

'I bet she would,' Loma replied.

'She is well-known for being secular and westernised like us. The new wave of Sunni and Shia do not agree with our beliefs or our way of life.'

'I cannot disagree with you.' Disappointment showed on her face.

'Now, back to action. There are many ways to flee the country. Selma did. I have heard she joined her son somewhere either in Jordan or a Gulf State.'

'Did she? Where did she get the money from? I know that she was skint.'

Soad recalled the old feud between her and Selma.

'Do not worry about her. I know some people who could smuggle you to Jordan. It's the only country that will take in Iraqis now. Our passports are red flagged all over the world.'

'Yes, gone are those days when other countries used to roll out the red carpet when we used to spend holidays with open cheque books,' she said.

'For you maybe, but you need to have the cash to achieve an escape plan.'

Loma examined her Cartier diamond bracelet that Soad envied so much.

Their conversation referring to the good old days was short-lived when a deafening knock came on the door. They clutched each other in fear and touched each other's bodies with a firm grip, ready to plead for their lives.

'Open the door; you are wanted,' shouted a thunderous voice.

They stared at each other and shouted a desperate desire to hang on to life. The attackers tried to break down the front door. As the noise became louder the couple became more terrified.

'Let's go to the back of the house; there is a small service door that overlooks the other street,' said Loma.

'But what if they see us. I got myself in trouble because of you. I will open the door,' Soad screamed.

'Please do not; they will shoot us,' Loma replied, but Soad became louder and louder with insistence in response to the demands of the intruders.

Loma ran and tried to pull Soad with her, but the latter resisted, thinking she would be safer if she betrayed her friend to save her own skin. She rushed to the old maid's room and urged Soad to accompany her.

'You go ahead, my daughter. I am an old woman who is done with life. It is no life anyway. Please, you go ahead.'

Loma felt that her urging was in vain. She could not get her thoughts together because of the noise, anxiety and turbulence. It felt like an earthquake. Just then, Loma felt her grip on the old lady's hand loosen. Her survival instinct prevailed. She dashed to the rear of the old house to avoid confrontation. With difficulty, she tried to find the service door keys among her deceased mother's clutter. The door was locked. Then it sprang to mind that her mother used to hide the keys in the drawers in the adjacent room. Once she was old, she had become increasingly forgetful as her memory betrayed her. Loma opened the first drawer with no success, then the second. The third one was lucky. It was difficult to unlock the rusty, unused lock until she heard screaming and shouting which spurred her on and she managed to open the door. The fresh evening air made her feel alive. She ran into the street bare-footed and aimless pursued by noise — a combination of shouting and shooting. Loma blocked her ears with her fingers.

Chapter Three

Escape from Hell

The situation had become dire in Baghdad. There seemed no end to the civil war and no limit to the bloody scenes. Families were divided after having inter-marriages and liaisons at a time when religion played a minor role, if any in their lives. Most of the population was guided by a herd mentality directed by clergies and religious ignorant men who pretended to be leaders. Their main aim was to safeguard their own interests in power and money. Some had to change tack and follow the new order either to protect themselves or to reap some benefit from the generously thrown money derived from oil or from the US led government to ascertain some control in such chaos.

Closer to the Tigris River in al-Adamiyah stood a huge mansion. The relatively newly refurbished house sat beside the river. Malaka's house, which she bought for a pittance from the daughter of an Iraqi ex-prime minister in the 1950s, who was on the verge of bankruptcy, saved Malaka from prison. She bought the house at a bargain price from a desperate woman who was keen to flee Iraq at any price. She knew that Malaka had her eye on the house, and she would get it either with a little money or by accusing her of treason because she was vulnerable as a result of her association with the previous era.

It was a cheap price to pay giving Malaka a hefty discount if it facilitated her exit from the country without her being questioned by the authorities. Serving the old regime was a thing of the past, she needed to work smarter to adapt to her new circumstances. With a well calculated move, she deserted her old house, which was the home of her activities, namely prostitution. But her business had expanded beyond that to reach further afield into other countries. She bought factories, houses and boutiques, not only in Iraq but in adjacent countries such as Jordan and United Arab Emirates. Her adaptation skills were unlimited. She sat and remembered old memories over a cup of sweetened Turkish coffee. She had started working with her mother as a cleaner at affluent Baghdadi houses where she sexually serviced lonely and desperate soldiers and labourers, worked herself up the ladder, and endured the abuse from pimps and clients alike until she became a prominent madam servicing the old regime with amazing rewards. Sex and intelligence go hand in hand.

Since the US invasion of Iraq, she had rebranded herself as a business woman and was ready to work with the devil if necessary to achieve her goals — power and money. She opened new channels with the Americans and provided them with important intelligence about the old regime. Likewise, she was building bridges carefully with the insurgencies and the new government personnel. Her work as a double agent was not easy and it was risky, like walking on a fine thread that she could fall off at any minute.

She had to sacrifice some of her working girls by reporting them to the extreme Islamic groups. No one knew what happened to the poor, helpless girls. Her act was to pretend she had an allegiance and commitment to Islamic and religious principles.

'If Napoleon and Stalin, did it; why not me?' She was referring to Napoleon Bonaparte, who executed his Egyptian mistress and prostitutes to satisfy the angry Egyptian mob when he invaded Egypt. He was opposed because he was considered an infidel. He also took this action to protect his soldiers from diseases carried by gypsy prostitutes, according to the tales. History repeated itself during the Bolshevik revolution era in Russia.

Malaka's new contacts with the external powers, Americans, Iranians and Gulf States, helped her to rebrand her business with lucrative rewards. However, satisfying men's lust continued to be the centre of her business. She worked as a mediator between all parties if the need arose, and she used her influence on men. For instance, those who needed permission to travel or even a pardon from any party, she procured at a hefty price, either in cash or for other favours. Her shrewd thinking stemmed from experience in that trade during her early life hardship and made her an astute business woman with a keen sense of danger and gain at an equal level.

'I will work with the devil if I have to,' she once said.

Her huge newly refurbished mansion had been renovated in a tacky way according to the previous owner's friend and neighbour who once commented that no one could keep up with the massive costly maintenance of her house. She once commented when she was sitting by the swimming pool at the Al-Elwya Club, 'Malaka's refurbished the house depicts her vulgarity and lack of taste.' Those harsh words were conveyed to Malaka faster than the velocity of thunder. The poor woman paid a hefty price for her words and spent some months in prison.

The country's dynamics were the same as they were in Saddam Hussein's days. All that had changed were the faces and there were too many of them to know who was a friend and who was an enemy.

The landline phone rang early in the day. The maid responded and approached Malaka who was immersing her plump body in a new modern bath.

'Phone for you, Ma'am,' the maid said in Arabic with her apparent Assyrian accent.

'I have told you hundreds of times, not to disturb me while I am bathing,' she shouted as she turned her body with difficulty because the bath was narrow.

'I know, but I had to break the rule because her name is Loma.'

The name made Malaka jump from the bath and expose her saggy boobs and her un-noticed private parts covered by her protruding belly.

'Hand me a towel and ask her to wait.'

The maid left the bathroom in haste with a smirk on her face. She had gained her mistress's trust because she had picked up the rules of the game so fast.

Malaka rushed to her bedroom from the ensuite to dry herself before she put on her bath robe. The maid entered with the wireless handset in triumph. She loved to watch her mistress in a state of anxiety — one never witnessed before, even in the darkest days. It gave the maid a sense of control. She handed over the phone and left the room, but not without trying to overhear some of the conversation.

'Alo, this is Malaka.' Her false greeting could not hide her anxiety.

'Hello, it is Loma,' said a faint voice full of fear.

'*Ahlan*, nice to hear from you. Where are you?' Malaka gained confidence from Loma's weakness.

'Thanks, I am somewhere in Iraq,' she replied in a fainter voice in an attempt to hide her identity.

'Iraq is too big, dear. I hope your family is well?'

'They are indeed. Thanks for asking. Karim recommended you to me to arrange some business.' Loma was vague on purpose.

'Of course, I think he mentioned it in passing.' Malaka adopted an indifferent attitude in the hope she could get a better deal out of the bargain.

'And?' Loma hissed.

'I think we need to catch up to finalise the deal. We cannot discuss it by phone.' At that point, Loma realised her conundrum with Malaka, who never behaved in a straightforward manner. She could only hope that Malaka would agree to all her conditions to secure a safe exit from Iraq. On the other hand, she knew she should be super careful and not disclose her whereabouts. Many Iraqis were victims of kidnapping for a handsome ransom or death by accident. A word from Malaka to whichever party meant a hefty ransom on Loma's head. She knew that she would be worth more if Malaka wanted to sell her to any party in the conflict. The only card she could play was the fact that her husband and his family were recommended by a prominent Gulf Sheikh. His widow, Sheikha Hasna was a very influential figure known for her charitable work in the Middle East, and Malaka would never dare to upset her now that she had expanded her business abroad.

'I understand your situation, but you need to know about my critical position.' Malaka tried to keep her voice quiet so her maid wouldn't hear, knowing the high risk she would face if the maid used what she heard against her. More so, she wanted to protect Loma — the chicken that laid golden eggs.

'I'm glad you appreciate the situation,' Loma said with sigh of comfort.

'We are close, like a family, despite Selma trying to ruin our relationship. I could not forget your mother's kindness,' said Malaka.

Loma realised her sympathetic voice tone was not genuine.

'Then what is the next step?' she asked in a worried voice.

'Let's make Karim our contact and I'll give him another phone number to call. The travel arrangements should be in place soon.' Malaka showed off her power and control.

'Okay, then it is an agreement, and I will follow your instructions.'

'You will be fine, but do not forget your friend in the future.'

'No, how could I?' Loma produced her words with difficulty. Malaka was no one's friend. Her only friend was money.

Chapter Four

Under the Burj Khalifa Steps

Selma spent the first few days since her arrival in the United Arab Emirates at her son's modest flat in the Al-Sharjah principality. It was separated from the principality of Dubai by a motorway that was a few miles away.

The building was old and dated back to the 1970s era, when money was scarce. Since the late 1990s and the new millennium, skyscrapers had mushroomed around it and suffocated the small monument from the past in a relatively new country that had only gained independence from Britain in 1971. The rent for the flat was cheap, which suited her son, but Selma didn't like the place. She grabbed every opportunity to make disparaging comments about the flat, the street, and the neighbours who she called riff-raff or low-lives.

Her son had a job as a clerk at Dubai Harbour where he spent most of the day and sometimes part of the night working and leaving Selma alone. To start with, she was gutted by the lack of structure in her life and also the lack of social activity that she used to thrive on, but more particularly the gossip and undermining others. She had no friends, no contacts, no gossip and couldn't slag off others, which was the heart and soul of her life. She grabbed the opportunity to catch up with her son for gossip about someone who had come to UAE or someone they had met accidentally in the shopping mall, an acquaintance from the old days in Baghdad. She knew that a significant number of middle class and skilled Iraqis were flocking to UAE for a better life and more for safety, the same as she had. The threats to kill and kidnapping for a ransom or for political or religious affiliation were thriving in Iraq, and many Baghdadi residents would rather live in poverty in other countries than lose their nearest and dearest, or paying a hefty ransom they could not afford.

As the days passed, her son was promoted to a more responsible managerial position with better pay and shorter working hours. They had more time to rekindle their long-lost connection and they strolled in Dubai's malls, which were heaving with people of all nationalities from all over the world. The malls were where social life began and ended. The summer lasted too long with temperatures above 40°C and reaching 50°C at times with suffocating humidity. The air-conditioned malls were the only answer to such weather. They could shop, eat, and enjoy all the available entertainment, cinema, theatre and even skiing. Slowly and steadily during the day the temperatures outside climbed. During the evenings and nights, they benefited from colder temperatures enabling them to engage in outdoor activities.

Selma had a lot of news to tell her son about what had been going on in Iraq, Baghdad, the Al-Adamiyah district, family and friends, after all the years he had been away from Iraq. Many sad stories of people lost either by war, murder or accidents were discussed over the dinner table, restaurant or at a cafe.

'Please stop; I cannot bear it,' Ahmed shouted in a loud voice that turned heads in Cafe Paul in the Dubai Mall.

Selma was embarrassed by his unexpected reaction and held his shaking hand. She felt his extreme anxiety that added to his volatile personality.

'It's happening to all the Iraqis, dear. I bet all religious affiliated factions and ethnic groups suffered a great deal.' Her smooth voice had a calming effect on his mood. It was contrary to her usual inflammatory reaction to the slightest and simplest matter.

'I keep repeating we lost your father to alcohol. His liver could not cope anymore. I was terrified to attend his funeral and his burial ceremony at Al-Adamiyah graveyard because the fighting factions used it as bait and kidnapped or killed one another.' A huge sigh came from Selma — a bitter person who had suffered so much.

'Mind you, he gave you and me a hard time. We have peace since his death. Good for us.' His words were empty and without sympathy.

'I agree with you. I would not have been able to join you here if he was alive.' Selma uttered another sigh of relief.

'I could not cope with him if he had accompanied you here,' he said as he let out a long breath.

'You would have killed each other,' she said with huge confidence.

She sipped her espresso and gazed at the horizon — an immaculate design created by the best interior designers and architects, who had flocked from all the corners of the world to show their art work. She examined the mille-feuille cake on the table. It was a luxury because she could not afford to frequent the French-themed cafes in Baghdad for financial and security reasons alike.

'War is not all doom and gloom, dear. It is an opportunity to get rid of bad apples,' she said in a calm and soft voice as she gazed at the horizon.

'Who are the bad apples?' Ahmed had regained his need to gossip, slag-off and get satisfaction from the plights of others.

'Who else dear. Our lovely neighbour, Loma and others like her.' She smirked thereby declaring her satisfaction.

'Damn her. You know, I don't wish her death, because I want her to suffer.' His voice was full of vengeance.

'They have been pursued. Her husband disappeared. She was hiding from everyone and especially from me. The fool woman thought that I would grass on her to the Americans or the Iraqi authorities. Not in a million years. I do not want to lose the pleasure of taking my revenge by myself.' Her words were cemented with confidence as she thought about her goal and tapped on the table with joy.

'I've heard that her sons have arrived here and that they are doing well with lucrative jobs,' he said.

'Lucky, but bitches never die. Even so, I wish her well. I am ready to meet her now. I've heard that she is well connected with professionals and politicians in this country. No wonder, her son is going places.' Selma's smirk grew wider.

'Not even that. I've heard that she is connected to royalty in this country. But how can you find her?' he asked with a puzzled look on his face.

'She will not be far away. *The people who are alive may meet soon*, according to the Arabic proverb.' They laughed loudly to the astonishment of the cafe frequenters. It was an extreme change of mood.

Chapter Five

The Escape from Hell

A four-by-four Toyota snaked its way along on the almost melted tarmac as it left Baghdad in the scorching heat of July. The heat was exceptional, and the car's air-conditioning could not cope with the heat that left the passengers with only one option — to let the hot breeze from the open windows cool their sweaty bodies. Even so, the passengers were indifferent to the heat. They could hardly feel it.

The driver was an old Kurdish man, who spoke broken Arabic as he tried to chat to both the overtly anxious passenger and the mortified one. The middle-aged woman had covered her body from top to toe with a black *abaya*, which hid her prominent breasts, that were popping out of a tight T-shirt. Her jeans showed her fine, well-sculpted body even though she was approaching her late fifties. Drops of sweat were dripping from her long dark covering, but she felt the coolness of the breeze from the window like a door from heaven that opens to hell. She was escaping something of a much larger magnitude — the hell of war.

Loma felt that she had miraculously escaped the different militia checkpoints set up by all the different factions with different names but with ambitions and goals to take control of the country. Since the absence of State power and the national army after the toppling of Saddam Hussein by the US led army, whose control was limited to the oil sites, leaving the country meant heading into turmoil.

Loma had identity cards with different surnames to produce at the appropriate checkpoints, who had different political and religious affiliations. Her top to toe *abaya* gave her the perfect disguise, plus her seniority had the added benefit of deterring young fighters from searching a decent old woman. She had made a point of not wearing make-up and showed only minimal facial features. Also, having a Kurdish driver was helpful because the newly elected Iraqi president was a Kurd. Each time the car was stopped by young, frustrated men,

Loma sat and recited verses of the Quran. She had been even more against religion since the horrors of war started, and she sought help from anywhere possible. Every extra minute being alive was a bonus for her and other Iraqis. She watched with sorrow as the dead bodies mounted up in the streets of the capital — a city that had been once a safe and secure place to walk around at any time.

When a young man shouted in a hysterical manner and asked her to leave the car at one of the checkpoints, Loma pleaded with him.

'My son, I am an elderly ill woman and want to go to Jordan to get medical treatment. We have no doctors or medicines anymore.' Her voice was shaky and full of fear; it would be the last time she would be heard.

'You are a Saddam supporter, and you get the best treatment regardless.' He raised his voice louder.

'No, my son. Saddam killed my brother in the war, and I am a widow after the death of my husband. I can't find the medications since the embargo by the West hit us hard. Thanks to Saddam and his antagonistic behaviour towards the world.' She composed her words carefully to hide her fear of the soldier discovering her secret that her husband was one of those wanted by government officials led by US represented leadership. She was worried about falling into the hands of Iranian affiliated forces or even the Sunni insurgency. The plot was too complex and incomprehensible to Loma. It was a matter of survival. There was no one she could trust.

'May God save your mother.' Loma's begging tone softened his attitude.

'I lost my mother in the war. Our house was bombed by the Americans.' As he uttered his words his eyes were full of tears.

'May God give you the patience my son.' She tapped his shoulder and touched the strap of his rifle.

'May God be with you,' he replied ignoring the driver's papers that verified their identity and ushered him to move. A big sigh came from Loma and the driver.

The driver did not stop once during the fourteen hours it took until they reached Turabil, the border compound between Iraq and Jordan.

Here they were interrogated again, but it was conducted more lightly. The officer had received a fax from the Jordanian Ministry of the Interior. 'Let her in,' said the Jordanian soldier as he stood and saluted her with an official military salute much to the driver's surprise.

The driver then drove faster and spoke to Loma in broken Arabic.

'Welcome to Jordan. You are very welcome.' He believed he was carrying precious cargo.

Loma took off her *abaya* with a big sigh as if she had been born again.

'I hope so,' she replied quietly.

Chapter Six

The Precious Discovery

Selma woke up from a deep sleep after endless sleepless nights at her newly rented flat.

Her son, Ahmed, had upgraded their accommodation after being promoted at work. He was able to climb the employment ladder with hard work, even though he was often put down, he made the necessary connection with friends, but at times there were enemies too. His work was mainly import and export between China and Iraq via Dubai, and he had mastered it well.

The rent was reasonable at Al-Sharjah, the poor sister of the next-door Dubai, where the rents were sky high after the rush of immigrants from all over the world. They filled job vacancies that had arisen because of the explosive expansion of business in the city. Since cash came from all over the world there were unlimited investment opportunities and plenty of prospects were offered by the principality such as free land lease and cheap Asian labour. The change provided prosperity for everyone. The stability of the political atmosphere was another factor that attracted capital from the adjacent unsettled countries in the Middle East.

Building had extended to Al-Sharjah and skyscrapers had grown close to the seaside and the interior alike in an area that once upon the time had been a fishing village.

Selma stood on the balcony of her flat that overlooked the sea and watched the waves. There was a fresh breeze before sunrise. Scorching heat would come by the middle of the day. She was left with no choice but to be incarcerated inside the tiny flat where she fanned herself under the cool breeze of the air-conditioning. Her son would have to leave early in the morning in time for the first shipment from Basra in Iraq.

'I wish Basra would disappear,' she said to herself indicating that she thought it was a problem. It was her usual curse when she wanted to dismiss anything she disliked while she boiled eggs for her son.

'No Mummy, we make a living from it and after all it is a marvellous city,' he replied in haste as he munched a piece of bread with a slice of sheep feta before leaving the flat. Selma turned her head as she heard the door shut. She rushed to the stairs, pulling at her transparent nightgown that could not hide her bulging stomach. 'What about your eggs? The sandwich will be ready in a minute,' she called out as she walked part of the way down the stairs.

He climbed back up the stairs to grab his egg and pickled mango sandwich like an obedient pupil waiting for instructions from his strict headmistress.

'You forgot something.' She pointed to her right cheek to remind him to kiss her. He obliged with a hasty shallow kiss much to her discontent. She believed it showed his lack of devotion and interest. She wanted to be the centre of attention as she had always been in the past. She shuffled up the remaining stairs.

'I think old age is catching up with me,' she said to herself.

The young Kenyan maid started cleaning the floor of the flat with the vacuum cleaner, but Selma has never been satisfied with her quality of work. She picked up a magazine from the pile next to the telephone. She examined it with indifference. *Zahrat Alkaleej* was one the well-known Emirati woman's publications produced in the oil rich principality Abu Dhabi. She called the maid to bring her coffee to the balcony. Her tone was full of authority and rudeness. She sat on the lounger turning the pages without interest, glancing at the latest fashions; how to match outfits with head covers to achieve a colour-coordinated outfit. She sighed because she found it difficult to cover her hair completely. She recalled what she said to a friend when the *hijab* had become a social necessity after the invasion of Iraq and the takeover of the hardline attitude, 'I would never put a rag on my head.' She had uttered the statement without caring that it might humiliate stanch religious believers. But, hey ho, she had to wear it even in her advanced age and because of her religious Muslim background. By wearing it she wanted to gain respect from the locals and also get protection too. She continued turning the magazine pages until a photo stopped her. She examined it thoroughly and shouted at the maid.

'Bring my reading glasses.'

The young girl came in no time carrying a silk pouch that contained silver-framed reading spectacles. Loma put on the glasses and scrutinised the photo. The face was familiar, but difficult to see clearly; it was as if she was gazing at an old Dutch painting. It was a small headline about a wedding party that took place last week. It was on the social pages where affluent families showed off their wealth and importance in society. She started to read in a loud voice that was mixed with the noise of the vacuum cleaner.

'Eman and Zaid, an Iraqi couple, got married at Rotana Hotel in Dubai.' *Aha, we meet again. It is Loma. The living will always meet again.* She repeated the old Arabic proverb in her mind. Then she sat upright as if she was waiting for a modelling shoot with immense confidence.

'Bring me the phone,' she bellowed rudely to the maid. The maid came with the phone and Selma did not bother to thank her. She dialled her son's phone number, which she knew by heart. The call went to his answering machine.

'Alo, guess who is here. Loma is in this country. Yes. I want more information about where she is and what she is up to. Everything and anything.' She disconnected the call with a smirk and repeated the proverb yet again, this time aloud. 'The living will always meet.'

Chapter Seven

A New Life

On a bright day in early spring when there had been no distinction in the seasons apart from mild winter weather and a very long hot in summer, Loma walked with a relaxed step in Al-Sharjah fish market. She glanced at the nearby arches built in 2015, to replace the ancient ones. In the past the principality had relied on fishing and pearl collection before oil was discovered in neighbouring Abu Dhabi. It had benefited from the discovery of oil since the union of the Emirates principalities after independence from Great Britain in 1971.

Loma was accompanied by her daughter-in-law, Huda. The shopping list was fish for a seafood feast for her two sons and their families. Since she had arrived in UAE, she had been living with her eldest son, his wife and her grand-daughter.

After she had bought the fresh seafood, she began thinking about cooking Iraqi recipes. The best one come from Basra in southern Iraq. She remembered cooking this for her best friend Sheikha Hasna in London. Her old connections from the past had been helpful. She felt the need to be thankful to those who had welcomed her since she set foot in UAE. She had been in touch with her old friend Sheikha Hasna, and received a warm welcome as they re-kindled their long-lost friendship. Loma was indebted to her for saving her life and arranging her escape from Iraq. She knew that she would never have escaped without Hasna's influence.

Loma thought back to the early 1980s when Hasna's husband had been the Emirati ambassador in the UK. Loma's husband had been the military attaché at the Iraqi Embassy.

The two women met and shared trips to their favourites, Harrods and Harvey & Nichols, to satisfy their shopping addiction at the expense of the government at the time. Loma had helped Hasna to improve her English, which she had learnt back home at a time when girl's education was restrictive in the 1960s. However, her father was progressive and a strong believer in educating women in his up-and-coming country. He used his influence as a prominent sheikh, and he became a minister in the newly formed government after UAE independence. He stood firm against religious clergy who objected to educating girls as a move to westernisation, which they believed might taint the local mentality and culture.

When Hasna learnt about Loma's plight and her need to escape the brutality of the civil war in Iraq, she helped her flee the country and saved her from the bloodbath that was taking place. Since the early death of Hasna's husband from cancer she had devoted her life to her four children and charity work to help women become independent and to help deprived children all over the world. Her children were now grown up and had found their way in life with exclusive jobs in politics and finance. Her two daughters had married high-society husbands. Hasna felt that she should be faithful to her late husband's memory. She knew love had faded away a long time ago, but she honoured the commitment. She was subdued by her culture and devoted herself to her family. She had never thought of marrying again despite the eligible suitors who had approached her following the death of her husband. Her commitment spread to her work, which she found fulfilling.

It seemed that Loma's sudden entrance into her life was like lightning on a dull day. She has insisted on hosting her at her grand villa at Al Jumeirah Beach since her arrival in UAE. They spent the days chatting, sipping Arabic coffee and reminiscing about their days in London, Paris, Baghdad and Dubai. Hasna felt sorry for what Loma had gone through because of the war. They continued their friendship after Loma moved to live with her son. Hasna was a hundred per cent loyal to her friend, which was why she had used her important family connections to negotiate a decent and safe exit for Loma from Iraq. The conversations about their families, lost husbands and work were unlimited. Hasna also admired Loma for standing by her husband, Riaz, through his life, despite all the adversity and his disloyalty to her. She was a feminist and believed in women's empowerment and that they should take control of their lives. Their culture dictated that a wife should stick to the husband regardless of the circumstances. Their conversations about husbands, their families and memories were endless. Loma had to stay with her eldest son according to tradition as he was now the head of the family.

Loma returned after Hasan's numerous generous invitations. With her hazel eyes she examined her son's modest three-bedroom flat. It is not bad for a recently arrived immigrant, but it was not to a princess's liking.

Nevertheless, Hasna insisted on eating with her at her son's flat. She remembered Loma's delicious cooking — *mutabbaq samak* — fish cooked with rice and saffron or turmeric, if you could not afford saffron. Loma insisted on getting the best Iranian saffron to welcome her best friend and saviour. She was spoilt for choice. She turned to her daughter-in-law, Huda, who was not very helpful; she was not happy with her mother-in-law for infringing on her freedom and living with her and her husband even though Loma did her best not to interfere in their lives. Huda found one excuse after another to disappear or to have less interaction with Loma and Loma easily had picked up on her unwelcoming vibes. Nevertheless, Huda, agreed to have Hasna for dinner and even volunteered to drive Loma to the local fish market. Having important contacts was vital in this country.

While Huda was strolling aimlessly in the fish market in a deliberate attempt to distance herself from her mother-in-law, Loma chose her preferred *zubaidi* fish, which is a kind of moon fish species that she had not tasted for a long while. The fish was available in the Persian Gulf. She remembered the days they used to get special deliveries of the even more expensive version of this fish which thrives in Shatt al-Arab, the huge stream where the Tigris and Euphrates Rivers meet at the sea. Loma woke from her daydreaming to the shouting of the fish vendors who were from different Asian countries. She tried to haggle with one who spoke in broken Arabic, but she could not beat him down. Her attention was fragile; regardless she turned her focus to getting the essential spices and ingredients.

Loma looked around for her daughter-in-law. She had vanished. Loma panicked because she was not familiar with the environment. Then, from the crowd, a face emerged. It gazed at her in anger with its hazel eyes and medium to large nose and bleached hair sticking out from under her head covering. She recognised her daughter-in-law, Huda.

'Why did you leave me?' Huda's tone was brimming with anger.

'You left me. I bought the fish and was looking for saffron when I realised that I had lost you.' Loma stuttered. She was fearful of her daughter-in-law's rage.

'You are an embarrassment. Let's go.' Huda turned her back on Loma and stormed off, much to the surprise of the shoppers and the vendors alike. Her rudeness was plain to see. A female bystander extended her hand to clear the way for Loma to follow her angry daughter-in-law. Loma thanked her and tried to catch up with the young, angry Huda who marched with a fast pace to the car park. Loma was confused about which one was Huda's car. Her brown eyes wandered as she scanned the cars hoping she would recognise it. Just then she heard squealing brakes. She narrowly avoided a car coming in her direction. The cold coming from the ice in the bag to preserve the fish, made her more alert.

'Get in.' Even the angry voice of Huda was a comfort after her anxiety of getting lost.

The car went past swiftly into the vast Al Wahda Street, one of the main streets of the small principality. The two women did not utter a word. Loma felt the need to burst into tears.

Why should I endure all this? Her inner thoughts were louder than Huda's shouting. She had realised that she had no choice in the matter. But she did have a choice in her life. A constant question played in her head like a broken record. Independence was, and always would be her mantra.

Chapter Eight

Having the Good Life

Selma started her day by checking her Facebook page, looking for lost and forlorn contacts, the ones she liked and disliked. The latter were the major category on her tick list. She wanted to know what they were up to and their whereabouts. She was also excited to spend some of her spare time looking for recipes to surprise her son with new dishes that she could adapt and integrate into old middle-eastern recipes. But most importantly she wanted the latest gossip from within the Iraqi community in the Emirates and other parts of the world. Her curiosity was about old friends and enemies. The transformation from one to the other was common. She gave advice regarding residency, divorce, accommodation, love affairs and never hesitated to give sexual counselling to women much younger than herself. Her advice or her wisdom branched off to include tips about the strict rules of residency, which were strongly linked to work permits, that made the welcome in UAE temporary. Mothers could automatically obtain a permit to stay if their children were in full employment. She pretended to be an expert but gave the wrong advice. She could rest assured that her son's employment was safe for the time being. She was proud to think of herself as a link between the locals and the Iraqi expatriates to master the use of social media so she could be in control of as much as possible.

Selma continued to be in contact with her daughter who lived with her husband in the United States of America, after having a short affair with a US solider in Iraq, before she fled abroad after being chased by the local insurgency who accused her of collaboration with the enemy. Now, she was married to young man and had become a United States citizen since she had obtained refugee status there because her son's father was American. Since she became a citizen, she had been giving Selma a hard time. Her daughter had limited resources and couldn't travel because her husband didn't provide well enough for her.

Selma put aside her bitter memories of the past and returned to the more comfortable reality. *One problem out of my way*, she said to herself in gratitude that her daughter was cared for even if her husband was useless.

It was time to focus and regain her previous glamour and power and stop slowing down.

She recalled the first time her son had explained how to use social media and email.

'I wish the dead could wake up and see how the world has changed,' she said timidly in a voice full of anxiety. Now, she was a master of that technology or so she thought. She could not deny she had sleepless nights because she was concerned about whatever was left of her extended family with the news of killing in the streets of Baghdad, plus the lack of or non-existent security after the fall of the Saddam's regime. Selma was tormented by horror stories about children kidnapped for ransom and the dire consequences that followed as she read Facebook pages. Her body was shaking. The maid entered.

'Madam, what shall we prepare for lunch?' she asked in broken Arabic. Her voice was quiet and timid to shield herself from Selma's unpredictable change of mood and bad temper. Selma glanced at her briefly. 'My son will do the shopping and I will cook, but I need you to be my sous-chef.' Her words came with a high level of confidence that terrified the poor maid. Selma was planning the dinner menu and would be inviting Sadof, the bitch as she used to call her. She was a relative who she disliked after hearing that she wanted to stop her marriage forty years ago to her deceased husband, Hasan, by trying to convince him that Selma was a low-life. Flashbacks of his death in the hospital from alcoholism replayed and the horrible events of burying him as mourners — family and friends had to run away under a shower of bullets from unknown fighters. She wondered how love and marriage could have such a sad ending.

She woke from her daydream to see Loma's name on the main Facebook page. It seemed that Loma had accepted Selma's invitation. Most likely accidentally, she assumed. Photos of Loma and socialites in Dubai struck Selma. *Bitches never die.* One photo was of Loma accompanying Princess Hasna to an art exhibition. She scrutinised the photos for comments. *Sheikha Hasna opened the new exhibition accompanied with an Iraqi old friend,* it said. That headline was a main article in a prominent women's magazine. Selma had heard of Hasna's influence and power and her respected position in society among both the locals and the immigrants. Knowing someone like Hasna would open many closed doors for her. She would not face any problems with a residence permit or struggle to find a job. 'The bitch Loma has fallen on her feet,' Selma whispered to herself. She dialled her son's phone number again. She had already called him a few times that day. This time he answered.

'Guess what? I found out information to die for,' she said.

'What Mum?' he replied with indifference.

'Loma is here, and she is rubbing shoulders with the elite of society.' Her sarcastic tone alarmed Ahmed.

'Bitch! I know one of her sons is working here; I hate him,' he said with apparent disgust.

'Never mind. Let me at them,' Selma said with confidence.

She knew he was in a rush to end the call. She could tell from the tone of his voice.

She searched through old messages and texted Loma. *Hello, long time, no see. I am looking forward to seeing you.* Selma waited for a response impatiently. *You will not escape from me. The mice cannot play around when the cat is present,* she thought with a smirk.

Chapter Nine

Working Woman

It was six o'clock in the morning in early June on the outskirts of Dubai, in the exclusive area of Jumeirah Beach. Loma opened the sliding door that led to the balcony overlooking the sea from the flat she could afford to live in with her son's family having a decent combined income. The sea breeze was saturated with humidity and the temperature was already in the early thirties and would reach the forties soon. She took a last deep breath of the fresh air knowing that she should close the door and switch on the air-conditioning. She sighed as she thought of her homeland and what was going on there. She switched on Arabic Al-Jazeera TV channel to be tormented with bloody images of people suffering in the civil war in her birthplace. At that moment a harsh voice spoke.

'Don't you think others are asleep?' Her daughter's-in-law's brisk voice brought Loma back to the real world.

'I thought the school bus would arrive and your son needs to be ready,' Loma replied in a calm tone.

'I know how to manage my son, thank you.' Huda's moods were ongoing for one reason or another. Since Loma had fortified her ties with elite society via her close friend Sheikha Hasna and she had been recognised by the Emirati and Iraqi community alike, Huda had lowered her aggressive attitude towards Loma, but her jealousy had been doubled when Loma had been appointed as a special personal assistant to help her friend *the princess* run her charities. Loma's hard work and efficiency in completing the tasks was exceptional. She was so efficient that Hasna had promoted her to a chair president of her charitable organisation and increased her salary accordingly. It is not an act of nepotism as many of the Iraqi ex-pat community believed, but the result of her work ethic. Regardless of her professional success, the reduction of financial pressure could never fix the mixed-up family dynamics.

At first Huda was pacified when she considered the benefits she might obtain from the relationship with her mother-in-law and the elite, but she could not hide her hatred of Loma. Loma remembered her son meeting Huda and falling in love with her while he was studying political science at Baghdad University. Huda was the envy of society when she married the son of Riaz, who held the highest rank. He was the favourite boy of Saddam Hussein, and consequently the most privileged. It meant that she and her family would never need to worry about any financial difficulties and all their needs would be fulfilled. But alas, her lottery win did not continue. She came from a less privileged background, considered lower class by Loma and her family. Loma had no objections, but equally she had no influence over her estranged husband, Riaz, the father of her sons, to bless such a reunion. Huda believed that Loma could have done much more to help cement the marriage. Her suspicions had been confirmed by Selma, whose habit was to add fuel to the fire when they met at a social function in Baghdad.

'So, you are Loma's daughter-in-law. You are pretty. I think you are wasted to be related to such a witch. She is arrogant and has bad-mouthed you and your modest background family on several occasions,' Selma said to Huda. Selma's words continued to resonate in Huda's head for a long time and reaffirmed her dislike of her mother-in-law.

Huda left the flat without saying goodbye to Loma who was trying to dial her son's number, but it was busy. He worked early, and at times very late. Her anxiety and her urge to protect her family had increased since the recent disturbing events back home.

While she was sipping her hot, strong tea the phone rang. She pressed the button to answer with hesitation. She heard the voice immediately.

'*Al-salamu alaykum.*'

'*Al-salamu alaykum.*'

'I am Abdu, her highness's driver. I will come and collect you at eleven.'

Loma realised the time had been slipping away and she was a working woman. She rushed to switch on her laptop to study the sheikha's timetable and scheduled activities. She had to manage the staff and check the charity's financial status. Her head was spinning about where to start and where to end. She had impressed Hasna and gained her confidence and made significant savings in many areas since taking over the post. Loma controlled the money. There were ongoing fraudulent and unrealistic claims by employees and other agencies. She also had to rearrange the workforce. Before there had been too many employees who had no obvious role at the charity trusts, and then there were the expenses claims. To start with, she had struggled with technology. She had identified a huge gap in information technology knowledge including the use of the Internet and computers. She'd had no need to work with this in Iraq, and Iraq was sluggish in catching up with the rest of the world because of the embargo imposed by the West on it, following the invasion of Kuwait 1990. Her son and even her grandson were her main source of help. She also took an IT course to learn the basics not long after settling down in her newly adopted country.

Loma longed for financial independence and wowed she would not be dependent on others particularly her estranged/deceased husband or her sons, and men in general. Getting this job was her golden opportunity not only from the financial perspective but to boost her self-esteem, confidence and independence.

The time was 10:30. 'I better get ready,' she said as she walked to her bedroom. She approached the mirror and gave a big sigh as she examined the deep groves on her forehead. They were getting deeper. 'If only youth would come back one day, so I could recall what old age did to me,' she quoted an old Arabic poem. *But never give up.* She dashed to the wardrobe and took out a golden box of Dior make-up, a gift from Hasna for her birthday. She glanced at her face and the increasing lines around her eyes. She tried to apply her make-up with modesty; having entered the grandmother stage of life, a certain amount of decorum was required. The rose lipstick would match her olive skin, according to the beauty expert at Dior in Dubai Mall. The dark foundation was a must to hide the dark circles under her eyes and equally the lines around her mouth and in front of her ears. *Maybe Botox would do the trick?* So many women her age and much younger were using cosmetic intervention in Dubai, and surgical facelifts, nose jobs and liposuction. She examined the black mascara and put it back in the make-up box. *Maybe too heavy for me.*

She looked at her smartphone to keep an eye on the time and to see if the chauffeur had texted her. While she was replying to his message, a text message sprung up from Facebook.

'Oh no, not again!' Loma shouted. She was mortified and started to shiver with fear. Her hand was shaking so much that she dropped her mobile. She took a deep breath after reciting a verse from the Quran to calm her nerves. Then she picked up her phone with a shaky hand to view the message that had upset her. The message had been sent by Selma. Loma realised that she must have agreed to Selma's request to communicate by mistake. The damage had happened, and it was too late. She could not read the message without the assistance of her reading glasses. It was as if she had forgotten the Arabic language.

Hello. Long time. The fate of those alive is to meet again. Loma understood what Selma was up to by quoting the Arabic Egyptian saying. *You cannot run away from me. What is going to happen next?* she asked herself. Loma felt her body had become heavier despite her slim waist and lightweight frame. When she let her body fall into the chair next to her, she felt the pain in her back and a current travel all over her body. She realised the past would follow the present, regardless.

Chapter Ten

The Summit Meeting

Days went by and Selma was mingling with the Iraqi expatriate society successfully and using her false charm to subtly disclose secrets she happened to know. But she could not break through the local Emirati facade despite becoming accustomed to the local culture, which entailed less mingling with the other sex. The men put on a front, but she knew that the women ran things. Selma was aiming to beat her forever rival Loma, by being the first to have exclusive dominance over powerful local personalities. It was a big deal to be associated with the wife or the mother of a powerful and influential man. And she couldn't tolerate hearing any good news about Loma or even looking at her photos in the local magazines or on social media. She felt an urgent need to gather more information about her rival's contacts, activities and movements to build a strategy, but she needed to plan it carefully. Worst of all, she was not coping with the humiliation from Loma. Selma thought that she had extended her hand with an olive branch but had received nothing but rejection. After posting her request to catch up on Facebook, Loma had blocked her and given no response whatsoever. It was the final blow. Selma would never accept success without triumph.

'How dare that vulgar, low-life insult me like that,' she said to her son over dinner.

'She's a bitch and we should have dished out her dirt back home,' he replied in an angry and threatening tone as he hit the wooden table with his fist.

'Things were not on our side. If you remember how much I suffered. She arranged to have me locked in prison and you posted to the frontline during the war.' Selma behaved like the victim.

'No need to remind me about that whore and how much our family suffered because of her.' He threw the spoon on the table to the ground with a fierce force to exhibit his anger.

'And to add insult to injury, she declined my invitation on social media.' Selma's tone was full of desire to take revenge and to add fuel to the fire. There was a long pause between the two. But Selma could not waste time on it anymore.

'Listen we need to get even deeper to the heart of the Iraqis and the local social circle,' Selma said as she gazed at the blue sky through the window.

'But you are already well connected,' he said with astonishment.

'But not to those who are connected with Loma. Do not forget, the bitch has reached the elite of this country in no time. We need to mix with the likes of her and even the same people. I need to get involved in charity work,' she said with a grin.

'And since when is charity work of interest to you?' He lifted one eyebrow in puzzlement.

'Well, from now on, dear ... from now on.' Her smirk became wider.

'It's easy dead. You can call any of the organisations—'

'No, only specific charities, actually there is one,' she interrupted him.

'What do you mean?'

'A charity whose patron is Sheikha Hasna,' she replied calmly.

'I've heard her name.' He wanted more information.

'Who does not know her. She is not only famous because of her bloodline, but because of her renowned charity work. She is not a national success but more regional in the Middle East.' She couldn't help showing off her knowledge in front of Ahmed.

'Mum, be careful. Do not mess with powerful people. Loma is not easy as we know her from the past.'

'Neither am I, dear. Neither am I, my dear. I have an idea about how to get into her life.'

'What do you mean?' His tone had become high-pitched out of anger.

'I've heard that she doesn't get on well with her daughter-in-law, Huda, isn't it?'

'Yes, it is. I knew her brother from the local shop and then from the army. They are a different class.' His words were said without him realising his mother's plans and vicious intention.

'Perfect. We have to meet our old dear friends to make sure that they are comfortable and hope they trust us. We are a friendly family, aren't we? Her laugh resembled a witch in a horror film.

He reciprocated with his own laugh, an even worse one. 'Mum, I think the devil would be wary of you.' They laughed again, this time in unison.

Selma munched her small piece of naan bread with apparent distraction. It was not food for her thoughts and plans. She crumbled the bread. Her son came to her rescue. She smiled. 'We are always a good team,' she said.

'Good one, Mother.'

Chapter Eleven

For a Good Cause

Life goes on and people carry on with what they do, regardless. Loma carried on her daily routine, spending her day between her office or at Princess Hasna's favourite charity where she cared for abused, deprived children who had been uprooted from the war-torn Middle East. She was summoned to present facts and ideas to the devoted and selfless princess who was making up for her emotional void after the loss of her husband, the love of her life and her rock in the social map in society. She had forgiven him for having a second younger wife, but she could not digest the bitter taste she felt that she'd had to share him with another woman, despite her position as the highest in the family hierarchy and the first and oldest wife. Her two daughters were enjoying successful traditional marriages according to local culture. Her sons were settled with wives and children and had successful careers.

As soon as the office work was completed, the formalities were dropped. Loma and Hasna would catch up like good, old friends and reminisce about their youthful memories of London, visiting its tourist attractions, shopping at Harrods, and wining and dining at London's prestigious restaurants. They sat over strong, sugary cups of tea and *shabura* biscuits, well known in the Gulf region.

'You naughty girl. You made me drink the first glass of wine,' Hasna whispered as she looked over her shoulder, to make sure no one was listening.

'We were young and wanted to experiment.' Loma giggled at the happy memories.

'I told you, Baghdadi girls like you are more used to drinking alcohol than me. I am from a more conservative society. It would have been a big scandal if the news had spread back home.' Hasna's voice showed anxiety.

'I know, you were a good girl. Thankfully we had a near miss. I was really worried when a friend of mine came to greet us and she spotted us tasting French wines at Maxim's in Paris, during our long weekend there.' Loma was extra careful not to be overheard.

'Oh yes, I remember. She was that glamorous Iraqi friend of yours. I was tormented by the thought that she would pass the information back to London. My husband would have divorced me.' Hasna's face became paler.

'It's history. I heard that Sadof emigrated to the United States. We are off the hook,' Loma said, wanting to change the subject.

'*Alhamdulillah*. I thank God for becoming faithful to our religion and you are the same, I guess.' She turned to bite her biscuit. She was careful not to eat too much and gain pounds round the centre of her body. Loma knew Hasna had changed. Her olive skin was covered with layers of expensive foundation to hide lines that had developed over the years and told of a hard life. Her black eyes were lined by *Arabic kohl*. This spoke volumes about how beautiful she had been as a young girl. Nevertheless, no one believed she was approaching her late sixties.

'How is it living with your son and his wife?' Hasna asked to change the subject.

'Fine. Although I don't think my daughter-in-law likes me living with them.'

'None of them do. They follow western ways now. It is the same for me. I think we need to accept it and move on.' Hasna showed her liberal western face.

'I am keen to get my other son to UAE.' Loma put her request politely.

'Why not? Where is he now?' Hasna's face depicted her genuine concern.

'He fled to Jordan, but there is no work there and he might not be safe. The Iraqi community think he is somewhere in this country.

I made it clear to the Iraqi community, he lives in Abu Dahbi. I'm worried he'll get hunted by Iraqi Intelligence in Jordan.'

'What about your husband?'

'Husband? What is a husband? You know we separated a long time ago. We lived a double life. I've devoted my life to my children, and he has his mistresses and politics,' Loma replied.

'I'm not surprised he was going places during Saddam's time. Here, men get a second wife. But where is he now?' Hasna said.

'No news. Obviously, he did not make it, otherwise we would have heard from him.' Hasna held her hand. Loma felt the warmth.

'I am so lucky to have you as a friend,' Loma said.

'Likewise.' Hasna released her hand.

'I will call my cousin and he'll arrange for your son to come here.'

Loma was over the moon. She could not help standing up and hugging Hasna.

Chapter Twelve

Mingling in Society

The weather was getting warmer and warmer by the day. The Dubai residents were eager to make the best of the few days left of mild weather when they could go outdoors during the day before the long hot season arrived. Soon they would be restricted to indoor air-conditioned buildings and malls during the day to avoid the heat of the summer.

A picnic in the park was a treat. Families getting together was a common occurrence in family-oriented society. The families tended to congregate according to their native countries, similar language and culture. There was little mingling of the population at large. Activities were mostly indoors and between local families, who were related, or who had developed a long-term relationship. They were often called working visitors.

In Safa Park, a group of men, women and children were gathered on rugs spread on the bumpy uncomfortable ground. Some squatted while others were luckier and sat on folding chairs. The food on the rugs gave an idea of the different nationalities. Stuffed vine leaves, onion layers and peppers were the ingredients in Baghdadi *dolma*. Huge portions of *kubus* had come from Mosul in northern Iraq. There were minced-lamb kebabs and vegetarian *aruk* wrapped with the Iraqi *samoon* bread for the poorer people.

The noise of opinionated elderly ones who shouted because of hearing difficulties was apparent. Children, who at last had their freedom, were shouting after being released from small affordable flats with limited space to play.

Some of the mainly Iraqi groups were new while others had known each other from Baghdad days before the recent disturbing events. They spoke freely but were careful not to indulge in political or religious subjects that could divide their families as had happened in their country.

Men were grouped and introduced to each other. They were trying to impress each other with their credentials and history about success and achievements. Women mixed more easily and started conversations about children, qualifications for jobs and recipes. There was a lot of showing-off.

Two loud voices took over. Selma and Lubna, were chatting on the edge of the group and made no attempt to lower their voices. Both were excited to tell their stories about the last few years since they had last met. Lubna had fled Iraq earlier, almost illegally and managed to secure asylum in the United States. She had joined her well-established son who had qualified as a medical doctor and subsequently obtained a better contract in Dubai. Lubna preferred to live in a middle-eastern country such as UAE that had close ties to the West. She would get preferential treatment because she had United States citizenship unlike someone like Selma who held an Iraqi passport. After they had exhausted talk about the lost glory days in Baghdad, they started to discuss current affairs.

'I don't need to renew my residency in this country. I get it automatically because of my son's work permit at the American Hospital. Luckily, mothers follow their eldest son in the culture here.' Lubna spoke her words with pride much to Selma's dismay and envy. She was struggling to renew her residency. 'I must say I am privileged that my son's prestigious job gives me a permit.'

Selma looked down. Lubna knew Selma was not telling the truth.

'I've heard it is hard to get residency if not impossible with an Iraqi passport.' Lubna's voice was full of arrogance and superiority.

'Probably for many, darling. But there are always exceptions to every rule.' Selma threw her last punch in the boxing arena.

'Talking about the exceptions; do you remember Loma?' Lubna was certain she knew everything about her, but even so she still wanted to test the waters.

'Yes, is she the one whose parents used to live next to our house in Al-Adamiyah?' They both knew that Selma knew the address by heart, but they pretended otherwise.

'Exactly, she is rubbing shoulders with the elite.'

Selma could not hide her facial expression of disgust and envy.

'Is she here?' she asked as if she did not know or even care about her.

'She is indeed. She is a personal assistant and friend to a very important and influential local personality. Despite living with her eldest son and family, she is finically independent and cared for by her Emirati friends. She will never struggle with visa issues as others do.' Lubna's last statement was directed at Selma. She knew about her difficulties in getting residency renewal.

'Is she?' Selma said, then she bounced back. 'She was one of the old Iraqi regime's major beneficiaries and was exploiting everyone for her own benefit regardless of their country or its regime. Her kind of people are unprincipled.' Selma sipped her strong tea and looked at the flowerbed that might or might not survive the heat wave that was coming soon. She wondered if Loma would survive her rage.

'Do you have any contact with her?' Selma bit the bullet. Being pragmatic and extracting further information was like gathering intelligence before a battle.

'I've seen her at a function or two. She added me to her contacts on social media. There is the Iraqi forum group that organises events for Iraqi ex-pats. There's an event coming up at the *Al-Chalghi al-Baghdadi*. I like the idea of it now that I'm living in the West. I think it's nostalgia.'

'I bet it is.' Selma's thoughts differed from what she was saying. 'I've read about it; it's an old Baghdadi art. They used to play it for the caliphate of Baghdad at the time of the Abbasid Empire.' Lubna was showing off her knowledge of history to Selma's indifference.

'It's very informative. When is the concert taking place?' She made a mental note when Lubna mentioned the date. Next, she attracted the attention of her son who sat close to her. She interrupted his conversation with old friends.

'Please book for the following event urgently,' she said.

'Since when do you fancy that kind of music.' He raised his eyebrows in astonishment.

'From today, my dear. I adore that music.'

Chapter Thirteen

A Day at the Concert

It was Eid. It comes on a regular cycle but at different times according to the Islamic, lunar calendar. It follows the breaking of the fast of Ramadan and the pilgrimage to Mecca, which are both part of the five pillars of Islam. Tradition has it that Muslim women celebrate by wearing new clothes, exchanging food, presents and sweets. The women are expected to bake dough stuffed with dates or sweet nuts to be presented with tea or soft drinks.

It was a golden opportunity to meet and greet family and friends who hadn't been able to catch up for a long time because of the busy and hectic lives they led. Their social lives were active, and people made full use of public holidays. It was no different for the Iraqi community in United Arab Emirates. The busy lifestyle was similar to that in the West and even more so in a country with free working regulations that attracted business from all over the world, and made people lose contact with their loved ones.

It was also an opportunity for the entertainment industry to thrive. The Dubai Grand Plaza Hotel was getting ready for the upcoming Iraqi concert. Following the unprecedented success and profit they made the previous year with *Al-Chalghi al-Baghdadi*, the concert venue was attempting to hold a bigger event with more spectators this time. The musical group members were nervous about not performing in their native land and were in fear of religious fundamentalists' reprisals. Religion placed them in the category of the infidels.

The audience started to arrive in droves. Families and friends came to the event to show not only their interest in their cultural heritage but their wealth, latest fashions and cosmetic interventions. Some did not recognise their former friends either because they had grown older or undergone plastic surgery or had Botox. Jewellery was displayed in abundance; gold and diamonds they had smuggled from their home country or bought locally. The noise of bored children and teenagers who had to accompany their parents to the event was intense. They had no interest in what was going around them but were mesmerised by their mobile phones and the latest news on social media. They would have preferred to listen to contemporary Arabic or western pop music, if they had the choice.

Selma made a point of making a regal entry. She was dreading the idea that she would have to wear a *hejab* as others of her age did, and she wanted to avoid unnecessary criticism.

'I would rather die than wear it, but I have to,' she said to Ahmed.

'I bet you miss your alcoholic beverages too,' he said and laughed.

'Well, not so much after the pain caused to us by your alcoholic father.' She sighed as she recalled scenes from her abusive relationship with her late husband. The memories were painful. The shouting, beatings, foul language and even rape never left her mind. She remembered Selma saying that she was a nymphomaniac, so why should she complain about a husband with a high libido. She did not understand that he was manic and had been diagnosed with mental illness as well as alcohol abuse.

'Damn the bitch; how dare she say that. I will sort her out,' Selma murmured.

Ahmed recognised her distress immediately. 'Mother, what is going on in your mind?' he whispered to avoid others hearing.

'Nothing dear.' She was already scanning the audience looking for her prey. He did not believe her; he knew her like the back of his hand. A plot was brewing in her mind. Selma turned to him as if she were an old person and began to comment in a negative way on others' appearances and personalities.

'Look at that woman; what is she called, Nuha? Is she Iraqi or Syrian? What funny shoes. Are they cheap monk sandals?' she said. She laughed loudly to draw the attention of others. Then she slagged off someone else. She was a fast mover; like a lioness catching her prey. 'Is that Loma?' Selma's voice was overheard by the neighbouring spectators.

Ahmed turned and looked. 'Yes, the bitch.'

'Who is that woman walking next to her with that entourage of people?' Selma whispered with apparent envy.

'It is Sheikha Hansa, a very powerful and influential personality—'

'I have heard of her and her connection with Loma,' she said as she interrupted him abruptly.

'Look, Mother, I think the young girl who is sitting next to Loma is her daughter-in-law, Huda.'

'That is good to know, my dear. I need a breakthrough.'

'What do you mean by a breakthrough?'

'You will know, my dear and very soon.'

Chapter Fourteen

The Unexpected Meeting

Time went by and the best way to spend it in Dubai was by shopping, if you could afford it. The guest workers, as they were called, gathered in the prestigious designer's mall along with tourists and headed to Burj Khalifa Tower or Burj Dubai to look at the city from a high point. The mall dwellers who could afford expensive goods left loaded with bags bearing designers names such as Gucci, Yves Saint Laurent, Christian Dior, and Dolce and Gabbana. The poorer ones were window shopping with desperate sighs of disappointment, as they wondered when they would be able to afford those goods.

In a small cafe, Selma sat waiting for her son to finish work and collect her. He dropped her off early in the morning to spend her spare time window shopping until he finished work, which would be early. He tried to lure her to go to the Burj Kalifa Tower, but she had a height phobia. She sipped her coffee and watched the shoppers, locals and tourists alike, and tried to identify what they'd bought by making a wild guess what was inside the bags with the brand names. She looked at her smartphone, which she hated to operate and had to follow her son's instructions to make it work. He had sent her a message to say he would be a few hours late, much to her distress.

'Another coffee, please,' she called out to the Filipino waiter.

As the minutes passed, Selma sifted through her memories, the happy and the painful ones. She was concerned about her daughter's wellbeing and how she was coping with her new life in the United States after she received messages from her to say that she was having arguments with her husband. Just then, Selma turned in response to a touch and a faint but familiar voice. It was a voice from the past.

'How are you doing?' It was a woman with a heavy body and the prominent curves that were covered by a long black *abaya* worn by the senior local women. Selma had difficulty recognising her face with the extra layer of make-up and the dark kohl around her black eyes.

'Don't you remember me, Selma?'

Selma rewound her memories and jumped up from her seat.

'Malaka is that you? What has happened to you?' She could not believe the change in her appearance. Time and war had added years to her real age — and a lot of weight.

'Yes, it is me. You are witty and intelligent as always.' Malaka showed her usual skills of being a master in the art of flattery and her ability to seduce anyone from under her *abaya*. She was good at it. She used to wear it during her teen days when she cleaned houses in the *Al-Adamiyah* district in Baghdad, including Selma's-in-law's house, when they could afford her services.

Selma remembered the past when she used to look down on Malaka with disgust from her modest position in society and even more so after she worked as a pimp or a madam at her glamorous brothel during Saddam's era when Malaka benefited from the lavish spending of the old regime. Selma would never forget her humiliation when she had to work for Malaka and then went to prison because of Loma. Selma had received no support from anyone including Malaka.

She came back to the present from her daydreaming to the bittersweet reality of meeting Malaka.

'I did not realise that you were living in Dubai,' Malaka said to remind Selma of her past influence.

'I've been here for a long while. I've declined numerous invitations from my son to join him here. You know he holds a high position in an import-export company.'

Malaka knew she was lying, and she also knew how Selma had struggled to get an entry visa to the United Arab Emirates to join her son. Malaka was well aware that all Iraqis were heavily scrutinised by Emirati Intelligence for security reasons because of fear of infiltration by terrorists. It was next to impossible to get a visiting visa, let alone residency. Nevertheless, a mother would be prioritised. Malaka's envied her because she didn't have children.

'What about you, how did you manage your residency? To my knowledge, you have no children to care for you.' Selma's last statement was a dagger into Malaka's heart. It was shameful not to have children in their culture. A painful expression covered Malaka's face as she recalled how she'd had a botched abortion after becoming pregnant to the first and the only love of her life, Rahman. Her memories were sweet and sour. He was the spoilt son of a well-to-do Baghdadi family. Malaka used to clean their house. He promised her marriage, thus she submitted to his needs of the flesh. She would never forget the humiliation when his mother fired her. She'd been almost naked — in her underwear. His mother had caught her son in action, after she came back from a shopping trip. Malaka left the house in humiliation and scandal. It was the talk of Al-Adamiyah for a while. Soon after, signs of pregnancy emerged. Rahman wanted to take responsibility, but his mother wouldn't listen to her son's calls to rectify the situation by getting married to Malaka. She attributes her current pathway in life to that incident otherwise she could have become a Baghdadi middle-class housewife with a husband and a family. She never forgot Selma's reaction back then. She has stirred things up, spread rumours and bad-mouthed Malaka.

'Where have you been?' Malaka was jolted into the present by the sound of Selma's voice.

'Oh sorry, my resident permit is sponsored by local VIP personalities, darling,' Malaka said to make her jealous.

'I am not surprised. The likes of you will adapt anywhere.'

'Certainly, darling. That is why people beg me to do favours for them.' Malaka's confident tone made Selma suspicious of what she was doing in this country and how she had managed to climb the ladder of power. She remembered when she had begged her to save her son from being sent to the front during the war.

'I bet you are very helpful to others.' There was caution in Selma's tone.

'Certainly. Actually, I saved a few of our friends by helping them escape from Iraq during the current turmoil and it paid off.' Malaka crossed her legs, took off and dropped her *abaya* to demonstrate her powerful position and show Selma that she had the upper hand and was fully armed.

'I see. Do I know them?' Selma asked like a mouse approaching a cat.

'Of course, darling. She is your best friend.' The confidence in Malaka's voice drew more of Selma's curiosity. Selma's thought process went faster than its usual speed. She had no friends in this country. Let alone best friends. 'Who is that friend you are referring to?' she asked in a brisk voice.

After a short pause, Malaka decided to stop torturing her. 'Your friend, Loma. I got her out of the country safely in return for my residency permit in UAE. Nothing is a free lunch. Isn't that what the English say?'

Selma was shocked with Malaka's efficiency in overriding the difficulties in Iraq and UAE and she knew that she must have important contacts in this country. Her toned changed to a more friendly and submissive one as she tried to rub shoulders with her. 'I have no doubt about your kindness and caring attitude towards others. May I ask you something, dear?' She sipped her espresso coffee with a grin on her face while Selma thought about the need of having Malaka on her side in anticipation of coming hard times. She would be a useful tool to achieve her aims.

'I've heard of a nice Iraqi restaurant in Dubai. I want to invite you there.' Selma could not remember the name of the restaurant.

'Which one of them? I've been to most of them.' She was showing off her new wealth and fiddling with her fingers to show off the expensive diamond rings and she kept deliberately touching her diamond and gold necklace that adorned her saggy cleavage. The absence of the *abaya* from her shoulders showed a pink strapless dress that clung to Malaka's plump body.

'Then you choose the place since you are an expert,' Selma said although she felt disgusted deep down. How could she associate with such a tacky, low-life person, but she bit the bullet and went on. 'It's been good to see you.'

'Likewise,' Malaka said sharing the same amount of disgust, if not more.

'Let's exchange phone numbers,' Selma said.

'No need, my dear. I have your number. But I will give you a missed call so you can save mine.' She opened her Louis Vuitton brown handbag and took out the latest model mobile and was skilful in finding Selma's number and making the missed call.

After a short period of silence, Selma could not control her urge.

'Who sponsored Loma?' Her hesitant tone made Malaka feel like a queen with control of the steering wheel.

'You will know. All in good time.' Malaka felt she had the upper hand.

Chapter Fifteen

Another Turn of Life

The population of Dubai and the tourists were enjoying the mild night breezes of the early summer season, which was equivalent to a summer heat wave in Northern Europe. Families were walking in groups on Al-Jumeirah Beach, exchanging greetings, enjoying ice cream and gossip. The local families wandered along the sand with multi-generational members of their families mixing together to the amazement of some of the western tourists. The younger ones weren't watching their step and behaving to the dismay of the older ones who didn't like the modern way of living adopted by their grand and great-grandchildren. An old grandmother was recounting the difficult lives they had endured before the oil boom when they lived off the sea produce or the limited agriculture and had a scarcity of natural resources such as water. A younger girl tried to hide her indifference to her granny's statements with a shrug, thinking instead of the colour of a Chanel handbag, she was planning to buy or a catch up with her dates while evading the watchful eyes of her parents.

Loma joined the crowd after having a hard day at work organising an upcoming charity event to help children orphaned by the Iraqi civil war. The work came close to her heart and was a distraction from the flashbacks of the atrocities of war she had endured since her departure from Iraq. The extreme scenes of death and the bloodbath in Baghdad never left her mind while she was awake or asleep. She was hoping to meet her daughter-in-law and grandson for a meal but was disappointed to receive a text from Huda to tell her that they were stuck in heavy rush-hour traffic, and they would head back to her cousin's place for a sleepover in Ajman instead of joining her. It was a business trip. Loma had been looking forward to seeing her grandchild.

'Another lonely evening,' she whispered to herself as she watched the sun set from the peer at al-Jumeirah Beach and remembered her first and last love, Ali. What had happened to him? Was he alive? Was he happy with his family, his wife and children? Loma felt the heartache and was about to burst in to tears when her phone rang. She searched her designer handbag with a high level of panic as she is always expecting bad news. She pressed the button to answer in a reflex manner thinking Huda had changed her mind. It was Hasna.

'Hello Loma, are you free?' Hasna's voice was warm, relaxed and as comforting as ever.

'Hello, your highness, I am fine but alone. I was hoping to spend the evening with my grandson by the sea, but it hasn't worked out.'

'I hope he is okay. And how many times have I told you not to address me with titles. We are friends or more like sisters.' Hasna's warm tone was full of genuine affection.

'That is an honour, I have always thought of you in the same way.' Loma's spirits were lifted.

'Listen, we have a charity dinner at Burj Al-Arab Hotel, and I want you to accompany me.' Hasna's voice tone became more professional.

'How come? I am not used to such high-profile places,' Loma replied shyly. There was a short pause, followed by a loud laugh from Hasna. Loma rarely remembered hearing it. 'Do you remember when we went to Maxims in Paris? I knew nothing of western etiquette then and you guided me step by step with sheer patience and a lot of humour.'

'I do remember especially when you spilt soup on the posh waiter to the astonishment of the other customers.' They laughed loudly.

'Listen, I will send the chauffeur to collect you. Don't worry about clothes. It's a charity. You can use the suite booked in the hotel if you want to freshen up.'

The call gave Loma a lift. She took a deep breath and gazed at the horizon out at sea. 'What is life without good friends?' she said to herself.

Loma waited for a short time until a BMW stopped, and a young Asian chauffeur stepped out of the car wearing a well-pressed brown suit with a hat that matched the colour of his skin. Sweat droplets covered his thick eyebrows. They were caused by the heat generated from his hat. He saluted her. '*As-salamu alaykum.*' He avoided eye contact with her out of respect. Loma examined him from the corner of her eye. *What a handsome guy.* He awoke something that had died inside her a long time ago. Maybe from the last time she slept with her lover Ali many moons ago but never with her husband. The sweet days went through her mind. How he used to climb to her parents' roof-top terrace where they made love until the early hours of the morning when her parents used to spend the summer in Lebanon or northern Iraq in Kurdistan, to escape the Baghdad summer heat. Her thoughts moved on to the painful days when she became pregnant and lost her purity after the botched abortion and the attempt to mend her hymen membrane.

She woke from her daydream when the car stopped in front of the huge building that was the Burj Al-Arab Hotel. She realised that she was close to it in Al-Jumeirah, and she could have reached it quicker on foot than by driving in the congested traffic. The chauffeur opened the door, and it reminded her of her time at the embassy in London and what followed when her estranged husband had climbed too high on the ministerial ladder in Baghdad at the end of Saddam Hussein's rule.

I understand why some would crush another to get such luxury, she thought to herself.

A young white butler who spoke fluent English with an accent whose origin she could not comprehend, greeted her with a light bow and guided her to the first floor to the Sahn Eddar lounge where the VIPs would have afternoon tea. She spotted her friend and employer Hasna, who was surrounded by an entourage of different people with different nationalities, colours and languages. To Loma's confusion, she was not able to distinguish if they were working or socialising with the loud noise they made.

Hasna spotted Loma from a distance. 'Come here, dear,' she said quietly as she indicated that Loma should sit next to her. The rest of the entourage kept quiet and watched the favouritism that Loma received. Many of them were desperate to receive it from the princess.

'Please, sit down next to me.' Her tone was as official as any boss should be. Hasna spoke a few words to her entourage, who responded to her request, and she dismissed her audience. Then she turned to Loma with a big smile on her delicate features that showed an old beauty with olive skin on which she'd tried to hide wrinkles with the help of her experienced Lebanese make-up artist with reasonable success.

'How are you? I miss you. I'm sorry we haven't caught up for a while.' Her voice was full of warmth and different from the professional way she conducted herself in front of her employees and helpers. The waiter approached the women with a smile to ask what they wished to order.

'The usual please.' Hasna gave her order without making eye contact with the waiter.

'They serve nice high tea here,' Hasna said.

'To be honest, I've forgotten the life of luxury, but I'm happy where I am. I feel I am productive and working. It's one of the best times of my life,' Loma replied.

'I cannot forget when you invited me to have high tea at the Ritz in London.' Hasna giggled but kept a watchful eye to make sure she was not seen by others.

'How could I forget; we thought that the Ritz was mean with their frugal portions and afterwards we rushed out looking for a kebab shop.' They laughed loudly and broke the princessly protocol that Hasna should follow.

'Nothing stays as it is. We will all die one day,' Hasna quoted a verse from the Quran to prove that there is no eternity.

The tea arrived with trays of different cakes, sweets and savoury items that made Loma drool. She made sure she was a proper, well-behaved woman in front of others, particularly Hasna.

The waiter poured the tea into silver cups. Loma waited for the hot drink to cool down and also for Hasna to give her the signal to start the tea ceremony as she joked about it when she visited China a long time ago. Hasna sipped her tea slowly and Loma did too.

Loma was enjoying her tea when a familiar voice pierced her ear drums.

'*Al-salamu alaykum.*'

Loma darted her hazel eyes towards the source of the voice and saw a woman dressed in a flowery dress that was covered with an Emirati-style abaya. She directed her greeting towards Hasna who looked surprised.

'I am Malaka, at your service, your highness. I come from Hamid the Emirates ambassador in Baghdad, if you remember.' She picked up the princess's hand and kissed it.

'Oh yes, of course. I have heard about you. Hamid spoke highly of you.' She turned to Loma. This lady saved your life along with many other Iraqi friends of mine. Let me introduce her to you—'

The middle-aged woman with very olive skin and a large nose, that appeared to give her authority, interrupted her. 'Who does not know our lovely Loma. We were neighbours a long time ago. Weren't we?'

Loma had a frog in her throat. She could not utter a word. Malaka came closer and planted two kisses on her bewildered face.

'I am happy, Loma, that you know someone like her. I asked our ambassador to get you out of the turmoil in Iraq and that happened thanks to Malaka. Am I pronouncing it correctly?' Hasna could not hide her effort to save her friend.

'Whatever you say, your highness is okay.' Malaka's tone became subservient to please her new master. Before Loma could say a world, a young woman who was Hasna's personal assistant approached them. 'Sorry Ma'am, there is an emergency at home, and they need you now.'

Hasna panicked in case her mentally ill grandson was in crisis. She rushed out and followed her assistant muttering a few words of apology as she left the lounge.

Malaka came closer and helped herself to a seat.

'So, we meet again. How are you, Loma?' She smiled before she picked a small macaroon from the tray and started to eat it slowly.

'I'm fine or I was until a while ago,' Loma said angrily.

'Am I causing that much nuisance to you? I've always been on your side. I'm the one who arranged your travel. I am your saviour, my dear, according to her highness,' Malaka replied in a musical voice that showed her control and dominance.

Loma realised it was a trap that she'd fallen into. *What does she know? What are her intentions? She would not do anything for free.* She came out of her trance when Malaka ordered the waiter to bring a clean cup.

'Actually, I'm leaving soon,' Loma said nervously.

'So am I, darling, so am I. I'm busy woman. I'll take it easy. I'm not in any hurry. I miss you and your mother, bless her soul, was kind to me.' Malaka's sweet tone did not deceive Loma.

'What are you doing here?' Loma's abrupt tone annoyed Malaka.

'The same as you, dear. I fled the war. You see, humans are like a sheep herd; they go after food and safety. After all, we want to live.' Her response did not convince Loma.

'How come *you* know the Emirati ambassador in Baghdad?' Loma said in a voice to reflect that she thought Malaka was a low-life.

'He is a man, and I am here to serve men's needs. I have many clients, including your husband. However, we need to look after each other. I want to know Hasna better and I do not want any disturbing rumours from you or anyone else to stand in my way, or else.' Her voice was strong, full of confidence and threatening.

'But if she realises your profession a ma—'

'And that is what I do not want to happen. And even if it happens you should correct it. She trusts you from what I gather,' Malaka said as she interrupted her.

'I'm not sure if I can be of help,' Loma said in a high-pitched voice.

'I am sure you can and will. We can help each other. We need to keep quiet about our past. What if Hasna heard about your love before getting married, what would her response be? We need to bury our past and start afresh. I think that there is no harm in having a truce.'

Loma burst into tears. She could not get rid of the stain in her past life. She had done nothing but love and trust a man and they had wanted to fulfil their normal physical needs out of love.

Malaka stood up and addressed Loma. 'I am sure we can work together, my dear. We never suffered relationship problems before. Not like that bitch Selma who spread rumours about everyone.' Her tone was menacing.

'What is this to do with her?' Loma asked.

'Nothing dear. I met Selma in Dubai Mall. She is living here. She is the same old Selma, slagging off others. We might have a reunion one day.' Malaka adjusted her *abaya* and covered her saggy cleavage and her arms. She threw a kiss in the air. 'See you soon.' She dismissed the waiter who came with the tea cup.

Loma burst into another bout of crying. *Oh no, not Selma again.*

Chapter Sixteen

The Summit Meeting

Days went by with the same routine. This consisted of working, eating, sleeping and some entertainment if it was allowed. Those who were practising Islam observed Ramadan and felt the exhaustion after one month of fasting in hot temperatures approaching 50°C at times with severe humidity to complicate it even further. Those who adhered to Muslim faith observed the month while others pretended to refrain from eating or drinking in public out of respect or shame.

Ramadan was over, and *Eid* was there to enjoy with its generous three days of public holidays. People went out to celebrate the end of the month by feasting on sweet food and enjoying entertainment. Immigrants with Muslim backgrounds celebrated according to their native cultures. Hotels and halls were fully booked. The Iraqi community did not have the Al- Chalghi Al-Baghdadi concert again. Instead, they invited a famous Iraqi singer, much to the dismay of some as she was associated with the old regime because she used to sing at Saddam's family parties.

Many families came to listen to the ancient music. Most of the audience were Iraqis with some other Arab nationalities, keen on that kind of music. The women wore their best clothes and their best jewellery. Those over fifty wore a *hijab* to cover their heads. In the younger generation it varied. Some wore a *hijab*, others did not. Mothers paraded their daughters to secure a future Muslim husband for them before they reached their thirties when they would be doomed as spinsters. Children found it a playground without the discipline of their parents, and they spread their toys in a small room next to the main hall. Friends and family were catching up, chatting, gossiping, reminiscing about the old days that predated the bitter civil war. They tried to grasp the moment that resembled their days before they came to the hard reality of being an immigrant in a foreign country. Families gathered with friends at tables according to their class, political and religious affiliation and education.

Selma sat with her old friend, Mona. Her son, Ahmad, was hopping from one table to another, chatting, extracting and exchanging information before he was summoned by his mother again. He came to her with a report and an update on Loma, plus the latest events, news and scandals. She waited impatiently to hear about her.

Before the noise got louder, it became quieter when the hall manager welcomed them.

'Ladies and gentlemen, a special welcome to Princess Hasna,' he said. She was the unofficial patron of the Iraqi community, having helped many out of the misery of the war. The majority stood up for her, either out of respect and gratitude or because they hoped to use her influence and power one day. She was wearing a long Yves Saint Laurent dress, that covered her shoulders and cleavage well, and a matching head cover. Then there was a Cartier diamond necklace, with a matching gold bracelet and earrings, adorned with diamonds. She was greeted with strong applause that made her feel like a queen or a Hollywood star. Selma told Mona that she was elegant but a bit tacky. When Loma emerged from the crowd, Hasna gave her a hug, to the envy of many. This was a shock for Selma. 'The bitch witch is spreading her spell on VIPs like the royalties in this country. She always falls on her feet,' she said to Mona but was heard by the adjacent table. Ahmad rushed to her. 'Mother, have you seen, the bitch is going places?' He was breathless.

'I know, dear. But I wonder what if the sheikha will find out about her past; what will the future of their sisterhood be then?' Her words came from a mouth with a smirk.

'Not to worry, Mother, I have already revealed some of the truth.' His tone was full of revenge.

'Be careful. She is well supported. We need to infiltrate to the princess's entourage and then expose Loma.'

The music played loudly; men, women and children danced cheerfully until all of a sudden Selma felt a hand touch her shoulder. She turned to see Malaka. 'Hello, dear. Are you enjoying the music?' Selma was startled. She seemed to appear everywhere.

'Please sit down. How are you?' Selma pointed to the empty seat next to her with some hesitation.

'No change since I saw you in the mall. Actually, I have met Loma.' The two women glanced towards Loma and Hasna.

'She is going places. She doesn't waste time, does she?' Selma's vindictive tone matched Malaka's big appetite to extract more information.

'So are we, my dear. I want you to meet Sheikha Hasna.'

Malaka's words fell like a thunder from heaven on Selma's head. 'Yes please, let's go now if possible.' Selma jumped up from her comfy velvety seat.

'No rush; all in good time.' Malaka's voice was calm and controlled to make Selma submissive. She finished speaking and glanced at Loma who had spotted them some time ago but was pretending to avoid looking in their direction. Selma's fierce glare pierced Loma who sat next to Hasna. Loma felt anxious, worried and angry. So much so that it showed and Hasna asked her if she was okay.

'Yes, thanks, a bit tired,' she replied. Loma tried to avoid looking at Selma, but she could not keep her out of sight. 'I am well, thanks. I think I suffer from an allergy,' Loma continued after a few seconds.

'What kind of allergy?' Hasna asked.

'I'm not really sure.' She kept watching Selma. *What is she up to?*

Chapter Seventeen

Lethal Contacts

It was one p.m. on a very hot day in mid-summer in Dubai. The fast-food outlet in the centre of town was a magnet to visitors and Asian labourers. They loved the cheap fast food that often consisted of fried chicken and chips. Asians came from countries such as Bangladesh, Pakistan, India, and the Philippines. The restaurant was almost empty and would be filled with regular customers later in the day.

In a far corner almost hidden in the fast-food outlet, far away from the sight of others, two women had tried unsuccessfully to disguise themselves with badly fitting clothes. The middle-aged women might have reached their sixties, but it was difficult to tell as they were hiding the lower part of their faces with face cover *kumars* and their bodies with *abayas*. It was not the usual sort of place they frequented. Their dress code was meant for senior local women who would never frequent such a place under any circumstances. The two women were sipping cold drinks and eating fried chicken to the bewilderment to the rest of the customers. They were talking seriously and did not realise how loud their voices had become. They spoke Arabic with Iraqi accents, Baghdadi to be precise. The discussion became increasingly heated, and the volume increased.

Selma and Malaka had planned their disguise so they wouldn't be seen meeting in public. They didn't want to meet at their home addresses for fear of being watched. Malaka's intelligence sources told her that this was highly likely. She had used the skills she gained from training and real-life experiences while working with Iraqi Intelligence during the previous era. She knew she was under surveillance by many parties with whom she had engaged in the past and the present.

The women could not help getting emotional.

'I need your help,' Malaka said.

71

'Ha! Me? How can I help you?' Loma said as she pulled a face and shrugged her shoulders.

'Loma.'

'What about her?'

'She is a bitch,' Malaka said with frustration.

'Tell me something I don't know. Out with it. What did she do?' Selma had run out of patience.

'She is trying to block me from getting to high-profile people in this country.' Her words came out like steaming anger pouring out of her nose.

'At last, you have been stung by her vicious venom,' Selma said, triumphant that her assessment of Loma was correct.

'I need your assistance to get Sheikha Hasna on my side. I did not realise how powerful and what a well-respected figure she is in this country and abroad. Also, I've heard she is kind and generous.'

'And you want to get a share of the cake,' Selma said.

'So do you. You can sort out that bitch and put her in her place. You have the will.' Malaka's eyebrows went up. Her latest Botox had been unsuccessful.

'You are capable. You are a professional ... well ... Madam had dealings with governments and security whereas I am decent society lady.'

Her words were challenging, but Malaka swallowed the insult and humiliation from Selma to get to her final aim. 'That's why I need your help. You are an elegant and well-presented lady. You are accepted in all the high-society social circles. No one could dismiss you, not even Loma. I am a mere ...' She spoke more slowly with a pitying tone to pet Selma's inflated ego and make her feel that she was in control.

'What am I supposed to do?' Selma took the lead in the conversation.

'I want you to infiltrate high society and get to Hasna.'

'But you were confident to introduce me to her at some stage. What has happened?' Selma asked.

'I thought I was, but Loma has warned her about me.' Malaka 's voice was full of anger.

'What can we do? That bitch is suffocating Hasna with her false love and warm friendship.' She screwed up her face in an attempt to degrade Loma.

'Well, information is power, and you have that in your hands,' Malaka said with confidence.

'Do you mean—'

'Yes, that is what I mean,' Malaka said by way of interruption.

'But you know it too. You can use it.'

'Yes, but no one will listen or believe me. Do not forget who I am.' Malaka lit a cigarette to the surprise of the Asian worker behind the serving counter, but she didn't dare challenge her for smoking indoors.

'So, when shall I start?' Selma waved away the smoke that Malaka had puffed in her face. Selma wanted to show her disgust at Malaka's lack of manners.

'Soon, very soon. We have time. I have got you an invitation to this charity event.' She produced a ticket from her Dolce & Gabbana grey leather handbag. 'You need to get to the women's hearts and minds, particularly Hasna.' She sniffed her cigarette triumphantly.

'Well, well, Loma. I will get you at last no matter how long the wait,' Selma hissed like a cobra aiming to spray poison on her prey. Selma extended her hand, and to Malaka's surprise she snatched the cigarette. She sucked it with force, and filled her lungs with smoke that gave her the lift she needed. 'Now or never. I am after you, Loma, as long as I breathe.' Her words were muffled as she exhaled the smoke. Her eyes fixated on the clean window as she watched a group of Asian men entering the take-away restaurant to fill their empty stomachs with cheap and cheerful food after a long hectic day. They threw a strange look at the women. Malaka smiled at the youngest bearded one and gazed at his private parts. He was touching himself and his private parts were bulging inside his fluffy traditional trousers. He knew she was a prostitute and he liked that.

Malaka laughed loudly after whispering to Selma. Then they both burst into laughter which caused other diners to stare at them.

Chapter Eighteen

Nostalgia

Los Angeles in southern Californian, is one of the most well-known cities in the world. It is the centre of the film and television industry, not only in the United States, but in the world. Since Hollywood's film industry kicked off in the early nineteenth century, LA has been a magnet to all talent, celebrities, and the rich and famous. It is the US city with highest number of Spanish speakers and there are also a significant number of emigrants from Mexico and other South American countries whose living conditions are often dire, in contrast to the immense wealth of others. Regardless, the city thrives even with such a huge divide.

In the Hancock District, in small house, Zelfa was alternating between listening to old songs from the Iraqi singer, Afifa Iskandar, to songs from the Greek singer, Melina Mercouri, on her old ailing CD player. Her taste reflected her mixed heritage.

She was preparing a hot meal for her husband, Jerry, who was enamoured with her cooking skills. The songs and the cooking of dolma reflected her cultural heritage despite the origin of the recipe being Turkish. She was proud of herself when she picked fresh vine leaves from her garden in the summer. Needless to say, the mild weather of California reminded her of her mother's native Greece, and she thought about the days when she used to spend holidays in Corfu, when she was a child, to escape the summer heat of Baghdad. Since she had escaped from Iraq and war, her life had been turned upside down.

Escaping Iraq meant liberty and more. Her daughter, Sheza, had been a reluctant concubine to high-profile politician's sons during Saddam's era. When Sheza reached her late twenties, she was made redundant, which was a relief to Zelfa. Even so, her chances of getting married and having a family were slim. Her daughter's role in a conservative society blighted Zelfa's life. She knew her daughter was seen as a high-society prostitute in the eyes of others.

When the opportunity came, she fled with her daughter in the dark of night to the north of Iraq without saying goodbye to her extended family. If anything, she was worried that her sister-in-law, Selma, would deliberately report her to the authorities either by gossiping accidentally or otherwise in front of the likes of Malaka. And this would have been the end of her and her daughter. She hid her mother's expensive jewellery inside her bra and stashed US dollars in her private parts, and she did the same with her daughter. The journey was like walking barefoot on spikes. They hired a four-by-four car and the driver evaded checkpoints on the route to Kurdistan in northern Iraq. Heavy bombing from Allied Forces provided them with some protection when the Iraqi soldiers, from Saddam's army, hid under the trees or anything that would provide cover. They were lucky to survive near-miss explosions one after another. The driver said he would not sacrifice himself for the two women but begging and seduction with some sexual favours changed his mind.

The journey that followed took them across the border to Turkey where they were helped by the sympathetic Kurds in the north of Iraq. After being interrogated by Turks, Zelfa gained entry to Turkey with her old Greek passport that she had acquired when she was young, although it did not provide her with access to European community countries as she'd hoped because it had expired a long time ago.

Luckily, Zelfa and her daughter were granted United Nations asylum. Not long after, Zelfa tried to call Jerry in the United States, but she received no response. She tried his mobile and landline phones, and even wrote letters when they lived in dire circumstances with Iraqi refugees on the Turkish side of the border, where they braved cold frosty nights and hot summer days with limited access to food, clothing and shelter. She was not very familiar with the new millennial communication methods such as email, which was banned in Iraq, but her daughter mastered its use.

After many months of miserable existence, they moved to the capital of Turkey, Ankara and then to Istanbul in very poor living conditions, where they shared accommodation with many others. Life was sombre and the women seriously considered returning to Iraq after having been rejected by Greece. Then they received a message through the United Nations office in Istanbul. It was from Jerry.

'Mother, come Jerry wants to talk to you,' Sheza shouted. Zelfa froze and could not utter a word.

'Yes mum, I have his mobile phone, see?' She showed her the number. Zelfa picked up her cheap mobile phone to check if she had enough credit to dial the number in the United States.

She pressed the digits with sweaty fingertips.

Jerry was as sweet as ever. His voice calmed her nerves. They chatted and she cried when he explained the reason for his hasty departure from Iraq without saying goodbye and he was alarmed not to be able to contact her for her own safety afterwards. He suggested he called her to save her the cost of a call. She found him sweet and considerate. She would have given up everything for a few moments just to be with him.

A short time later, he sponsored them and after months and months of waiting, they met him at Los Angeles airport, after flying via Europe. It was the time of her life to meet and live with the love of her life and she savoured it.

They had lived together ever since. Sheza continued to study economic science and had a part-time job as a waitress. She was living with her American boyfriend and had left her previous life behind.

Zelfa came back to the present when she heard the noise of a car engine revving. She looked out of the small kitchen window that overlooked the garage. Jerry was as handsome as always. He had put on weight around his abdomen and had more grey in his receding hair and fine wrinkles around his eyes, but he was sexy. She hugged him and gave him a warm kiss. 'The dolma is almost ready, darling,' she said as he handed her a glass of red wine. They clinked glasses.

'I have wonderful news for you,' he said. 'I'm being posted to the Middle East,' he said with joy.

'What? Where?' Her voice was full of insecurity mixed with fear.

'Well, I'll be based in Dubai, but I'll move around to different adjacent countries when necessary.' Zelfa realised his work with US Intelligence would take him all over the place. Since he had become the Middle East expert, he'd been promoted to senior supervisor for the middle-eastern operation to reward him for his work in Iraq.

Do I want to go back and live in pain again? Equally, I miss my people and the culture.' Her thoughts ran deep.

'What's the matter. You don't want to go?' His tone said he'd picked up on her insecurity.

'Well ...' She was hesitant to say what was going on her mind.

'You can stay here. You are a United States citizen. You're under the American authority's protection.' He raised his wine glass and through it he saw her green eyes and eyelashes covered with expensive mascara, her prominent nose and well-matched mouth. *She's still got it.*

Zelfa raised her glass. 'A woman should follow her husband wherever he goes.' Their glasses clinked again.

The delicious smell of the dolma cooking took over. Zelfa rushed to lower the oven heat in case it burnt. *I should never leave him alone. He will play around,* she thought as she examined him from head to toe when he wasn't looking.

'Darling, I will follow you to the end of the world,' she said. They clinked the glasses and said cheers.

Chapter Nineteen

The Unhappy Reunion

The scorching summer heat in Dubai had raised not only the temperature but people's tempers as well. Many immigrants brought part of their cultures to this cosmopolitan place. The Iraqi community was no different despite their caution about each other. They usually found a small space to interact and share the latest events. Some were waiting to emigrate to the western world, others preferred to settle in a country with a similar culture to their country but with western-world security.

The Iraqi cultural centre in Dubai was trying to bring back and revive many of the Iraqi literary poet's names, those who were alive or dead. And ones who were known for writing modern poetry. The liberal thinkers who had been sidelined by the intellectually oppressive previous regime.

Sheikha Hasna was the patron of culture or so she liked to be labelled because she had never forgotten the influence of the female Iraqi poets such as: Lamia Abbas Amara and the deceased Atika Al-Kazraji and Nazik Al-Malaika, who wrote about the liberation and emancipation of Arabic speaking and other middle-eastern women. Hasna had learnt their poems by heart when she studied Arabic literature at the University of Baghdad in the early 1970s. She remembered vividly the devotion of her family to her education and living in another country had broadened her horizon of knowledge and culture. Nevertheless, her will to learn had won the support of her father who believed passionately in women's education. She had become the patron to host literary evenings for the above poets and many others from other Arabic-speaking countries.

The Iraqi cultural centre could not ignore her effort and provided joint ventures to revive this culture which was disappearing after the

Allied invasion of Iraq and the meltdown of all the cultural institutions.

The evening at Rotana Hotel Hall was organised jointly between Hasna's office and the Iraqi Embassy. It was a women's event, and the audience was predominately local women who were interested in literature and culture. Many were from the Iraqi community.

The main hall was decorated with bouquets of flowers. Sheikha Hasna was wearing a long black dress adorned with golden embroidered flowers. Her head cover matched her dress, and it too was embroidered. She was wearing a Cartier necklace with matching earrings and a golden bracelet designed in a Bedouin style with a small diamond in the centre. She had tried to bring together the traditional and the new. Loma sat next to her. She was wearing a sky-blue dress designed by a local Iraqi designer and she had covered her shoulders with a black silk cardigan. Her jewellery was limited to her diamond wedding ring. She had made sure her Estée Lauder make-up was perfect and after the persuasive efforts of her girlfriends she was also wearing mascara.

'My make-up is okay, isn't it? Hasna asked Loma. 'My daughter bought it from Milan. Seemingly, Gucci is getting into the make-up game faster than the old French ones we used to use.' Just then, Hasna became aware that the microphone was not switched off on the chairperson's desk. She gave the Asian technician a firm look of disgust. He rushed to fix the matter promptly, but she could not hide her embarrassment knowing that the audience had overheard her remarks.

'Oh dear! It is switched off now. Not to worry. Normally I use Rimmel. It's cheap and cheerful, but not today. I have splashed out on a more expensive brand.' Loma giggled. Hasna ignored the joke. She felt insecure exposing herself to the public, but Loma had a calming effect on her with her soft smile. Then Hasna joined her with a light laugh that showed her bleached white teeth with her Hollywood smile.

The hall was full of women showing off the latest fashions from dresses to make-up to jewellery. The evening started with recitals of poetry by up-and-coming young female poets from different Arabic-speaking countries before moving on to the old names. After this, Hasna delivered her speech about the contribution of women's literature to the emancipation of Arab and eastern women. She emphasised how women's education would build the future society.

The interval was long, and the buffet was filled with Baghdadi delicacies from stuffed vine leaves — *dolma* to *quizi,* grilled lamb and rice, plus salads and other vegetarian food.

Loma and Hasna avoided mixing and eating with the crowd. They sat in the adjacent lounge chatting until the women had finished their food. While they were chatting, a woman entered unannounced. Selma was wearing a brown suit with a long skirt that had golden embroidery over a light, white shirt. Her make-up was immaculate despite her using a cheaper version of a famous brand. She approached the steps facing Hasna. Loma would not recognise her as her back was facing the entrance.

'Good afternoon,' Selma said in a gentle voice.

'Hello,' Hasna replied politely.

Loma turned and could not help emitting a sound of surprise.

'Selma, what are you doing here?'

'I must thank the patron of Iraqi and Arab culture, Sheikha Hasna for keeping such wonderful culture alive and introducing it to the younger female generation.'

Hasna picked up the conversation. 'You're welcome. Please sit.' She indicated the seat next to her.

'How are you, Loma? It has been long time since we've seen each other.' Selma's words totally shocked Loma. She was paralysed and unable to say a word. Her mouth opened, then closed. Selma had nothing to do with culture; she was an expert at destroying others' lives.

Hasna was surprised by Loma's wordless reaction. She turned to Loma. 'So, you know each other?'

'A long time ago, Ma'am. A really long time ago. Wasn't it, Loma?' She pretended to be friendly to keep the upper hand and did her best to keep the sarcasm out of it. Loma nodded, but her face was filled with panic.

'Loma's friends are my friends,' Hasna said joyfully.

Selma was prepared well with all the information and the necessary knowledge to steer the conversation from literature to make-up and fashion. Hasna was mesmerised despite Loma's failed attempts to terminate the conversation on several occasions.

Then the event organiser approached Hasna. 'I'm terribly sorry Ma'am, we need to start again.'

Hasna's soft and friendly tone changed to a more authoritarian one. 'We will come.'

'I will try to find a seat at the front so I can pick up the pearls of your wisdom, your highness. I have to leave now,' Selma said as she stood up.

'No, you can come and sit next to me. I have enjoyed your company.'

Loma opened her eyes wide as if she'd been hit by lightning. 'But your highness, we have no space,' she said quietly as she tried to hide her dismay.

'There is, Loma. Please make sure there is a seat.' Hasna spoke softly but firmly, and her attention was focused on Selma. Hasna stood up and was followed by the women as she made her entrance into the hall. The audience stood up and applauded before the scheduled events continued. Hasna indicated that the women should sit down. She smiled softly at Selma. Loma was distraught. *What is Selma up to?*

Hasna started the second part of her speech which many attendees were not keen to hear after having a heavy meal, but they had no choice.

They wanted to show their host country that they had the equivalent of a *first lady*. Hasna was number *one* for now.

A woman was sitting in the last row wearing expensive jewellery with a golden beaded dress that had a low neckline. She wore heavy make-up and tried to hide her face with a shawl.

The fish took the bait. They do not call me Malaka, the queen of the night for nothing. A light but strong laugh came from her that drew the attention of the women around her.

Chapter Twenty

Reunion at Al Jumeirah Beach

It was eight in the evening at the end of July on a hot day. A large number of local people, matched by the same number of visiting workers and a small number of tourists were coming out after having compulsory incarceration during the hot daytime. Many had woken from their compulsory siestas to revive their relaxed bodies.

At Scalini, a high-end Italian restaurant, a select table overlooked the deep blue sea through a huge clean window. The fog seemed to blur the amazing view of the sea and there was a big contrast between the heavily air-conditioned cool air indoors and the scorching hot outdoors.

Two women were sitting at the table sipping chilled Chardonnay, served in Bohemia crystal glasses. The conversation was in Arabic, and it became louder and louder to the astonishment of those who could not understand Arabic. Most of the restaurant customers and workers did not speak Arabic.

Zelfa and Selma sat opposite each other, waiting for their order of seafood pizza to arrive.

It was a meeting after years of separation and lack of contact for many reasons such as losing track of each other and deliberate ignorance.

Zelfa's green eyes shone through the heavy mascara. Her make-up hid the fine lines on her forehead. Each line told a story of a plight and suffering but could not mask her beauty. She maintained a slim figure but was not as toned as used to be when she was the sporty girl who won prizes in swimming and a tennis championship in the early 1970s in Iraq. Her light-blonde hair was enhanced with expensive dye to hide the few grey hairs. She was over fifty, but she looked younger than her age in her yellow, chiffon, flowery dress.

Selma had tried relentlessly to regain her lost youth with multiple layers of cheap make-up, as well as surrounding her large hazel eyes with *kohl* to make them look even larger. She'd had limited success. Her red hair was permed and dyed and dangled freely over her broad shoulders. She covered her hair with a blue silk shawl when she went to and from the restaurant to demonstrate her respect for age, culture and religion and because of her new agenda of getting close to the elite of society.

'Darling, lovely to see you,' Selma said as she kissed Zelda's red cheek just before they sat down.

'Likewise. I have not heard from you for a long while,' Zelfa replied.

'You didn't bother to ask after us when we suffered because of the war. You left Iraq without letting us know. We never heard from you. Ahmed tried to contact you when your brother died, but I'm not sure why you didn't respond,' said Selma.

'I lost track of where you were. I lived a nomadic life, moving from Turkey to Greece to Austria, looking for Jerry. Me and Sheza were almost homeless until Jerry found us, and we got married. We waited for months and months living hand to mouth under the United Nations with next to nothing for support until we were granted a US visa via Jerry's sponsorship. We moved from one state to another. Do not forget you were cut off in Iraq, Internet was banned, and mobile phones were not available to the common people.' Her long and thorough explanation was of no importance to Selma and her facial expression indicated her disbelief.

'Well, the past is past, and the rest is history. You are the winner, Zelfa, so laugh at last.' She took a gulp from her glass of wine to satisfy her envy and thirst.

'I miss my wine. Nowadays, it is a stigma to drink and many of our old mates have to pretend to follow Islamic rules by not drinking. Guess who has went to hej in Mecca — Loma. She has accompanied a powerful local princess from this country to Mecca to perform a pilgrimage, so she deserves the honourable title of hejya' She laughed loudly and attracted the full attention of the restaurant customers.

'Has she? She's the last person I would have imagined doing that,' Zelfa replied in a quiet voice as she felt the embarrassment of her sister-in-law's behaviour.

'There are many others doing the same too. Let's face it, I do not dare to drink in public. And I am trying to get into that princess's entourage so I should be the perfect good girl,' she said to Zelfa before she darted a fierce look at the waiter to make him pour more wine into her glass.

'Your lives have been transformed in such a short time since Saddam's regime was toppled,' Zelfa said with some delight that she was not included.

'Indeed, to a degree beyond belief. Nevertheless, we bounce back. Thus, I need your help.' Her tone became more serious.

'You are a United States citizen and the locals in this country pay respect to westerners regardless their background, because they are under the protection of Uncle Sam. Moreover, you continue to be the girl who turns heads wherever she goes. I want you to get into high society circles.' Selma's words came out as an order.

'Listen, I'm a married woman and I love my husband. I have suffered a great deal to get where I am. Yes, Jerry is away at work, travelling all over the Middle East, but I am planning to devote my life to him.' Zelfa's response was decisive with no room for compromise.

'Oh dear, oh dear. And you trust men. They have you today and they will throw you away tomorrow. You have a short-term memory, darling. Remember when he abandoned you before and it was the same with the father of your daughter. Men are pigs. You need to think about yourself first. You have time to think.' She turned and looked at the deep blue sea.

Zelfa was not expecting such a reception from her sister-in-law. But what did she expect from Selma? She did not trust her, and Selma did not trust others. Zelfa closed her eyes and remembered how Jerry had cheated on her. *Maybe she has a point.*

'Can you be clearer about what you want?' Zelfa asked Selma.

'Well, I need you to access some information.' Selma could not disguise her request.

'You mean you want me to become a spy and who should I spy on? Zelfa asked.

'Well, let's say an informant. Information from your husband and his friends,' Selma replied.

'And if I say no?' Zelfa's reply came as a surprise to Selma.

'Of course, you are free to say no. No one can force you to do it, but if you do not work with us, then someone else will take over as usual.'

'Who is the someone else?' Zelfa eyes darted towards Selma's.

'Well, we are working for the same front, my dear. We need to survive and that is not possible without relying on a strong person from society who is either local or American, the latter would be even better.'

Zelfa was puzzled; she did not understand what kind of mission Selma was hinting at and what role she was being recruited to do.

Selma was aware of Zelfa's confusion. 'Look, life is already too complicated. You don't want your husband to know about what happened in the past. It's better to keep things to ourselves. I will let you know what you are supposed to do in detail soon.'

Zelfa had heard Selma loud and clear. It was like a threat, and she could not deal with more mess in her life such as there had been in the past. Selma's words awakened suspicions about her relationship with Jerry and the time she had caught him red-handed cheating on her. She would see what Selma wanted her to do.

'I do not have secrets from my husband.' Zelfa's response was defensive, but she was not willing to open a can of worms.

'I'm sure you don't, darling. But there are dark corners in our lives and it's better to keep them to ourselves. I'm not going to tell you what I used to hide from your brother and vice versa. Do you know I found out that he had relationships with men?' Selma statement came as a surprise to Zelfa.

'My brother! That cannot be!'

'Well, it's true, but I could not do much. In retrospect, I think it was wise to handle it like that. What would have happened? We would have got divorced and I would have had no qualifications to work. I'm warning you, not threatening you, dear. There is no need for him to know about you and your daughter's relationship with the regime. I understand he might be a liberal westerner, but his work with intelligence would be compromised.'

Zelfa reconsidered her priorities. There was no harm in introducing Selma at one of the US embassy parties or gatherings. She was working as a matchmaker, so to speak. She took a long sip of her white wine. It was running out faster than she thought. She asked the waiter for another bottle, by pointing at the empty bottle in the ice basket. An extra bottle of wine would be helpful. She knew her sister-in-law well.

She is a bloody alcoholic like her brother, thought Selma. At that moment a noise came from her smartphone indicating a mobile hone message.

How's things going? Selma read the message.

The fish almost took the bait, but we need some time. Be patient, Selma typed her response with her lips clamped together in a look of satisfaction.

Excellent, was Malaka's reply.

Chapter Twenty-one

Ordinary Working Day

Each day was growing cooler. Tourists were flocking to Dubai to take advantage of the golden rays of the middle-eastern sun with fresher air. Winter was equivalent to summer in the northern hemisphere, and it came with a guarantee of full sunny days. There might be the occasional shower that would disappear in no time. The traffic was building up after the arrival of the locals from their holidays abroad and the visiting workers who had returned from their native countries where they had visited their extended families and escaped the heat of the summer months and taken advantage of the school holidays.

Loma reached Sheikha Hasna's charity office early in the morning before the build-up of traffic. She was driving an old Japanese car that she was proud of having bought with her savings. Her concentration on the road was not the best. She'd spent sleepless nights worrying about her recent undesirable encounter with Selma. She had tried to block that woman from her thoughts but hadn't succeeded. Loma had thought Selma was a closed chapter in her life, but she was coming back with a vengeance.

As she drove, she could not stop her thoughts about memories in Baghdad. It was like a film trailer. She did not spend much time at her mother's place in Al-Adamiyah between her mother's death and fleeing the country. She had lived a solitary life at her husband's home with no physical or emotional attachment. Riaz spent the majority of his time with his mistresses and prostitutes in different places such as flats and hotels. That gave Loma peace of mind and kept him away from Selma's plots and gossip. Loma had felt lonely all her life. Living with her son's family made no difference. Her son was busy all day and night, while Huda ignored her and limited her grandson from bonding with his grandmother. Getting away from the war was easier than trying to run away from the past. She was haunted by Selma.

She reached the office, but flashbacks continued to play in her mind. Not even the strong Arabic coffee the porter offered her could help. Her dark thoughts were interrupted by her mobile phone's eastern music tone, which was more appropriate for belly dancing than for an office worker of her status. She tried to ignore it, but she could not when she saw Hasna's name on the screen. She touched the answer icon and heard the soft and gentle voice speaking in classic Arabic.

'Good morning,' said Hasna.

'Good morning. How are you?' Loma replied as she tried to hide her anxiety and fatigue.

'Fine, thank you. Sorry to disturb you. I just wanted to let you know that I am recruiting more staff since our charity work has expanded.'

'Thanks. You really are an excellent manager who can spot deficiency in the work force. I think we are the victims of our success,' Loma said with enthusiasm that matched her will to achieve. Also, she wanted to pet her boss's ego.

'I've noticed you are working hard, and I can see you are exhausted.' Hasna's voice was full of pride.

'I am at your service, Ma'am.' Loma felt the need to be an obedient employee.

'Come on. Do not call me Ma'am as if you are addressing the queen. We are friends. More like sisters.'

Her statement calmed Loma down. Loma giggled as she remembered how reassuring Hasna had been when she had told her what to say and do when she she'd been invited with her husband to the queen's garden party in the 1980s.

'When will the staff start and what is their role?' Loma asked.

'I will discuss it with you later. I'm busy and need to attend a family meeting. I'm concerned about my grandson's health and might accompany him on a treatment trip to the United Kingdom. I think the new staff will start today.'

'Oh, so quick.' Loma felt left because she had not been involved in the recruitment process.

'Sorry, it was a hasty decision, but I hope it was a wise one. Anyway, you know the newly appointed operations manager and I have selected that person because of you.'

Loma was puzzled. 'Who is he or she?'

'You will know soon. There are a few of them. Listen, I have to rush, my grandson is in the hospital, and I cannot think clearly right now.' Hasna ended the call much to Loma's astonishment. She was anxious about the unexpected change, but she hoped for the best. Loma knew that there was no need to discuss something minor such as staffing issues with her boss. After all, she could not object to staff who were approved by Hasna.

She rang the bell and the very elegant Lebanese secretary responded in haste. She was wearing tight jeans, and an equally tight T-shirt covered her enlarged breasts. Her make-up was the envy of other office women who asked her for tips every now and then.

'Nicole, could you please bring the documents regarding the placement of Iraqi refugee children.'

'Yes, of course.' She walked away skilfully in her stiletto shoes. Loma examined her figure and elegance, which reminded her of her own younger days when she used to spend the summers in Lebanon. *I was even slimmer.*

The Bangladeshi tea man arrived with a strong cup of tea served in a small glass cup called an *estekan*. Loma looked intently at the small cup. It reminded her of her days in Iraq.

'Where did you get this cup, Abed?'

'Ma'am, it is not me; it is the new manager. She insisted on serving the tea this way.'

Loma felt threatened by someone who had just started and was trying to change things without her approval. *How come she had started without me meeting her? She must be very special to Hasna.*

Abed picked up on her curiosity to know more and he wanted to score points by being ahead of the game. 'She is from Iraq too, Ma'am,' he said to impress her.

Loma was not impressed. It was usual that people from the same country or ethnic group could be rivals, which might not be helpful in getting the work done. The civil war in Iraq had increased the division between people according to their political, ethnic or religious affiliation. They could not trust each other. She pulled herself together and tried to be professional.

'What does the new manager look like?'

'She is a pretty lady. She is very fair considering she is from an Arab country. I have heard her speaking Arabic fluently. She is in the newly refurbished office next to the Sheikha's one.' He knew he might have said too much, but Loma found the information helpful. Loma gazed at the ceiling. Should she ask for her or pay her a visit? She opted for the latter, thinking it was better to be proactive and it would be good to come across as a modest manager and be able to drop all the office formalities. She had a few sips of her strong tea to energise herself before she walked to the door. Abed opened the door for her with a semi-salute.

Loma stopped by Nicole, the secretary. 'Do you know about the new employee?' Loma asked.

'You mean the head operations manager? Yes. Sorry, I thought you had met her. I'll take you to her.' Loma followed Nicole to a lavish office used by Hasna in the past. Nicole knocked on the door and Loma heard a voice full of confidence tell her to enter. When Nicole opened the door, Loma could not keep the surprise off her face.

'What are you doing here?' Loma's voice was sharp and loud.

'Hello, Loma. Long time no see. May I introduce myself. I am the new operations manager. In other words, your manager. On some occasions.'

Loma's legs shook so badly that Nicole rushed to hold her up. It was Selma. 'Bloody hell!' Loma stammered as she tried to hide her emotions, which were in turmoil.

Chapter Twenty-two

New Life, Happy Life

The fresh breeze that came from the sea gave Zelfa energy. She sat in Ayamna, a middle-eastern restaurant at the Atlantis Palm Hotel and gazed at the sea and the people around her. The hotel was built on an archipelago. It was an artificial island partially reclaimed from the sea and reformed in the shape of a palm tree. It was meant to be an architectural masterpiece.

The smell of the middle-eastern grill penetrated her nostrils and made her mouth water.

She had lost her mother when she was young while they were holidaying in her mother's native Greece. From then on, she had been raised by her maternal grandmother and lived a nomadic life between Greece and Iraq, until she finally settled in Baghdad after the death of her grandmother. She was neglected by her father who was too busy having affairs with the maids. Then, after her father's death, she went to live in her brother's household. Although Zelfa became the lady of the house, but she was given a hard time and treated with cruelty or ignored. She could not get rid of the Cinderella complex. Her early instability, namely the lack of love and care in her life, caused her to become an anxious, insecure adult. She thought meeting Jerry and fleeing to the United States would sort out her life, but nothing helped to boost her confidence or improve her self-esteem. Her love for Jerry was fading gradually. She had not been able to have children and Jerry seemed keener on younger girls. She agreed to relocate to the Middle East and make a new start in the hope of reviving her marriage, but then she found out that Jerry was having liaisons with younger girls and prostitutes when he frequented Dubai's infamous brothels. He did not respond to her begging and tears, and she felt she had to accept his behaviour if she was to survive. Her main concern was her daughter who was settled and had a good job in the United States. A peaceful life without hassles was Zelfa's main goal. Nevertheless, her past seemed to follow her wherever she went. Now, she was under pressure from Selma to collaborate with Malaka. Working with Malaka meant one thing — exploitation of others' lives and emotions but hopefully not their thinking.

She came back to reality after a gentle tap on her shoulder. She turned to see a familiar face that had become puffy. Heavy, messy make-up could not hide lines created by years of suffering and stories.

'Hello, darling. How are you?'

'Hello, Malaka.' She was wearing tight trousers that revealed her huge hips. And a T-shirt with gold printed flowers that showed her saggy breasts. She had abandoned the *abaya* in westernised places.

'Darling, I hope you are well. I miss you dearly.' Malaka bent her heavy body forward and kissed Zelfa's cheeks. Zelfa did not move and looked at Malaka with apparent disinterest.

'Thank you, Malaka. Yes, it has been long time since we have seen each other,' she replied in a quiet voice.

'You know dear, I adore you and your mother, bless her soul. She was kind to me when everyone else turned against me.'

'I'm sure that you would have sorted them out there and then.' Zelfa giggled.

'I was a poor innocent girl.' Malaka had a sheepish tone in her voice.

'I'm sure that you have not called me here to tell me your life story.' Zelfa's response was direct and abrupt.

'Be patient, dear. I want the best for you.' Malaka adjusted her voice to that of a strict military officer.

'What are you offering? I had enough from you back home; now what?' Zelfa poured out her frustration in one go. Her raised voice attracted the attention of other customers.

'Darling, calm down let's have lunch and then we can talk business. I think raising your blood sugar will calm you down or should I say

drinking a glass of wine will.' Malaka was aware of Zelfa's weakness
for alcohol. Malaka pointed at the waitress. The pretty Filipino girl,
wearing a blue uniform with a short skirt and a jacket, rushed to their
table. The girl approached the women with the menu. Malaka changed
her caring soft tone to a rude one as she ordered food from the young
waitress.

'We need the mixed grill platter and two beers and your best white
wine,' she rattled off to the girl without making eye contact. The
waitress tried to ask which wine and ran through the variety of the
European wines, of which Malaka had no understanding whatsoever,
and she put up her hand in a dismissive gesture. 'Just bring the best one.'
The poor waitress looked at Zelfa, hoping she would rescue her; Zelfa
did nothing.

'Sorry, I took the opportunity to give the order without consulting
you. I've been here several times and I know what is good and what is
not, especially for you and me,' Malaka added.

'I am sure you chose well,' Zelfa replied with indifference.

'Sorry if I seem bossy—' Malaka began.

'Listen, I have no time to listen to you babbling. Can we get
straight to the point? Selma asked me to meet you. What do you want?'

'Nothing but good things for you, dear. I know you had
connections with the previous Iraqi government, well, the newly US
appointed Iraqi Government is under threat. There are many of
Saddam's supporters living in Dubai and we need information.
Intelligence is gold.' Malaka put her hands on top of her Chanel
handbag and showed off layers of gold bracelets that covered both her
wrists. Then she grabbed a cigarette and began to light it, ignoring the
puzzled expression on the waitress's face, and the no-smoking sign in
front of her.

'You were part of the previous regime's driving force, Malaka, you
know them well. How could the new regime trust you?' Zelfa made

her point abruptly. A loud laugh came with a big cloud of smoke from Malaka's wide mouth that was enhanced with Estée Lauder lipstick.

'Darling, times have changed, so have people and I am no different. I will work with the devil if need be.' Malaka took a deep breath and inhaled the smoke that gave her a buzz.

'You knew everyone back then, why me?' Zelfa said with some anxiety.

'Darling, you are Zelfa, and not only that, but you are also a US citizen and your husband is a prominent American figure in intelligence and diplomacy and whatever else. You are the ideal socialite who will be trusted and respected by the local dignitaries, ex-regime figures and everyone. You are perfect for all parties, and you will not attract suspicion. But I am a misfit, just a madam to them after all. No respectable home will admit me during the day. Mind you, some are happy to do so after dark.' Malaka's sigh was loud to indicate her desperation and her anger at the way society was treating her. 'I am sure your husband is well trusted, and he is in contact with politicians from all kinds.' Malaka was careful about her the last statement.

'What are you suggesting? That I spy on my husband?' Zelfa's angry tone made the waitress come closer in case she had to intervene in an unpleasant altercation.

'No, dear. I bet he is in on the game too. We work for the same goal to support the Americans and the West in general.'

Malaka's speech calmed Zelfa down. Zelfa gazed at the horizon. 'There is nothing for a loser to lose,' she said.

Malaka smiled with triumph. 'You will never regret it, I promise you. Now, relax, let's eat and drink and have fun like the old days in Baghdad. I will explain later in detail what you have to do.' Malaka poured the vintage chardonnay from the bottle to the embarrassment of the waitress who felt humiliated and thought she is not doing her job properly. But Malaka wanted to show generous hospitality to her prey.

'And what if I refuse to work with you,' Zelfa said in a confident tone as she contemplated Malaka's face.

'Life is full of choices, but the clever one will pick the right one. Just imagine if your husband finds out that you are in contact with the Iraqi insurgency. The Americans are very disturbed by the opposition to their presence in Iraq and they are very well aware of the contact of the Iraqis abroad to support them,' Malaka replied.

Zelfa turned her face away from the sea view as she absorbed Malaka's words, which were a clear threat intended to destroy her.

'I have never been in contact with anyone, and you have no proof.' Zelfa put down the glass of wine forcefully.

'Darling, you have strong and living proof sitting next to you. It is easy to find or even make-up such evidence. It is part of our job.' Malaka pointed at herself and knocked back another glass of wine, then she laughed aloud as she enjoyed torturing her new victim.

Zelfa reacted to Malaka's loud laugh with a smile. *I have nothing to lose. I will pass information from here to there. After all, there are no secrets in the East. She will find out one way or another.* She watched Malaka becoming tipsy after a few glasses. Zelfa had abstained from drinking alcohol for a reasonably long while after attending Alcoholics Anonymous in California. They clinked their glasses. 'To new adventure and business,' Malaka said in a loud voice.

Chapter Twenty-three

Regal Tea

The weather was cooling down with the approach of winter in Dubai. The fresh sea breeze meant hordes of locals, visitors, families and singles, walked on the beach following months of incarceration in air-conditioned houses and malls. The younger generation found the opportunity to walk and mix with the opposite sex. Girls were chaperoned by a female unless they managed to escape for a clandestine affair. Older people sat in cafes or on benches or even on the ground overlooking the sea.

Overlooking Al-Jumeriah Beach was a huge villa that could easily have belonged to a rich and important person. The facade was painted sky blue to match the colour of the sea. The architecture was a mélange of art deco and traditional middle eastern with concave arches surrounding the doors.

The entrance was via a long driveway, and it took several minutes for a car to reach the main gate. The car park accommodated four cars. A car stopped by the large Indian-style mahogany, hand-engraved, wooden door. This was the main entrance that led to an enormous living room with smaller rooms branching off it. The large room was lavishly decorated with Bedouin silver artefacts that ranged from daggers to necklaces to coffee pots that sat on mahogany shelves. The room smelt of French wood polish. Along one wall were two designer pistachio-green sofas. Gold embroidered cushions were spread on the ground to mimic a comfortable Bedouin tent and provided seating for guests who preferred to sit in the traditional way on the ground. This was common with the older Emirati generation. In the middle of the room was a table on which sat coffee and teapots and a large variety of local and western pastries.

A voice full of confidence spoke in polished English. 'Please make sure my guests are comfortable,' Hasna said to her well-trusted Filipino maid. Hasna was on a mission to make her guests comfortable and to impress them with her generosity. She could never afford the stigma of being seen as mean or inhospitable.

Since Loma and Selma had commenced working together, Hasna had felt the tension between them. Loma was her long-term dear friend, but she taken a liking to Selma because of her sense of humour, jokes and mocking others using her acting skills. Selma was an old beauty, and her glamour only drew Hasna's attention to her good qualities. Hasna had planned, much to Loma's dissatisfaction, a catch-up over a cup of coffee with both women. It was to be an informal meeting for a reconciliation between the two or so she hoped.

Since Selma had commenced her work with the charity, she had been following a plan that meant she would not upset Loma in order to get closer to Hasna. She had been walking on egg shells. Loma fully understood what Selma was doing and knew that she intended to ruin her life as she had in the past. Loma had taken every opportunity to send a subtle warning to Hasna about Selma's vicious intentions and it was inevitable that there would be friction and confrontations. Hence, Hasna had decided to take the matter into her own hands and reconcile the two of them over a tea party at her place.

It was four o'clock in the afternoon when the doorbell rang. The Bangladeshi porter opened the door and greeted a tall, slim woman wearing a blue *hijab* that covered her dyed blonde hair. She was colour coordinated with the long sky-blue chiffon dress and she had covered her cleavage with a dark blue jacket. Loma was ready to score a point against Selma.

'Sorry, Madam will be with you soon,' said the maid much to Loma's disappointment.

Loma sat and gazed at the portraits hanging on the walls in the guest room. One depicted Hasna in her youth. She was pretty. The photo made Loma think about her life and wonder how she had ended up here. Her thoughts were interrupted by the sound of the doorbell.

She heard a familiar voice through the thick wall. The maid admitted Selma. She was wearing a dress overlaid with beads that did not suit the occasion. Selma had paid extra attention to her make-up. She had probably spent hours fixing it and changing it to match her maroon-coloured dress and lipstick that matched her precious Jimmy Choo shoes.

'Hello, dear. I did not expect to see you here,' Selma greeted Loma sarcastically.

'Me neither. I hope we won't have another turbulent meeting,' Loma said as she avoided eye contact with Selma.

'You always have bad intentions towards others. I am kind to you. Aren't I?' Selma raised her evenly threaded eyebrows.

'Time will tell,' Loma replied with indifference, knowing Selma did not mean what she said.

Hasna's cheerful voice broke the silence and created a short truce between them.

'Welcome both of you. So nice to have you. Please feel at home,' she said with genuine affection. The two women looked at Hasna as if they were two school girls summoned by the headmistress to await their punishment. They stood to greet her and kissed each other's cheeks twice. Then they waited for her to invite them to sit down. It was like having an audience with the queen. Loma had never followed such protocol. Her relationship with Hasna had been less formal, but she was guided by Selma to show respect for Hasna.

'I wanted to see you both together outside the work environment,' said Hasna. Just then the maid came in and poured tea for Hasna and Loma, but Selma asked for coffee.

'Please help yourselves.' Hasna pointed at the trolley filled with pastries and sweets. 'Back to our talk. I know you come from the same area, and you lived close to each other for most of your lives. I know you have some differences and that happens in the best of families, but at work I want you to be friends. More like sisters.' Hasna sipped her black tea. 'I have known Loma for a long time, and we are like sisters,' she added. Selma hid her disgust and kept a straight face, but this was short-lived when Hasna carried on. 'Despite knowing Selma for only a short time, we have clicked. I think of her as a family member.' Her words struck Loma like a sledgehammer. She was worried about the future.

'I want a promise from both of you to respect each other and try to work harmoniously. Selma has experience in managing businesses. She has told me that she ran her family business in Iraq.' Loma glanced at Selma, to send a message saying she was a liar. She had never worked a single day in her life. Hasna had been sucked in by Selma's lies.

'I want my charity work to be remarkable, not only in this country but all over the Middle East.' She spoke the words of a dreamer. Hasna rang the golden bell to call her maid to serve a second helping of tea. She poured the inky black tea into the small glass *estikan* and made sure not to spill it into the saucer.

'We have loads of work to get through, ladies and I will be relying on your effort and hard work,' Hasna said in a loud voice, yet she did not understand the degree of the divide or that the long feud between the two of them was too deep to mend over a cup of tea.

'Ma'am, I am at your service,' Selma said in an obedient, submissive tone not in keeping with her feisty and stubborn nature. Hasna gave Loma a look that indicated she wanted a promise or a commitment.

'Yes, we want to work together,' Loma said hastily as she was forced to comply. At that moment the maid entered in a hurry and whispered into Hasna's ear.

'Terribly sorry, ladies, I don't mean to her rude, but I must leave you for a family emergency. Make yourselves at home.' A deep silence descended on the room. The two women avoided looking at each other. Selma ate her chocolate cake and sipped her coffee, then she broke the silence.

'So, you do not like working with me?' She wiped the cake crumbs from her mouth with a silk napkin.

'I have not said anything. She is a sensitive lady and has sensed our differences,' Loma replied in a defensive tone.

'Do you think I like to sit next to you ... Ha! I don't like to sit next to crows.'

'Likewise.' Loma's reply was instant.

'I understand that you are her favourite. I wonder what would happen if she knew about the darker side of your life,' Selma said with a smirk.

'What are you talking about?' Loma said with evident anger.

'You know what I mean. Our history follows us wherever we go. You might have got away with it in a liberal society of the 1970s and 80s in Baghdad, but never here, my dear. Even if the princess is kind and keen to endorse you, her pristine reputation will prohibit her. And I will make sure she has all the information she needs.'

'You are evil; I hate you.' Loma burst into tears.

'Well, you will get used to me from now on. You have no choice.' Selma sipped her sugary coffee and made a humming noise as she prepared for the war.

'What do you want from me?' Loma seemed to give up after Selma had thrown down the gauntlet.

'Nothing, my dear, just be nice to me. I want to get into Hasna's heart and mind. I want to introduce our mutual friend Malaka to Hasna.' Selma smirked.

'Are you mad? No way! You know what Malaka is. There is no way that I could bless such a union.' Loma's breath came out like a Victorian steam engine.

'She is no different from some. Do remember that.' Selma's threatening tone came as a final warning.

Loma stared at the silver collection of Bedouin-style jewellery and daggers hanging on the wall. She wanted to stab a dagger into Selma's heart. *I have to comply with her rules. Let's consider it a truce, but the fight will never end.* Loma turned towards Selma.

'Well, it's mammoth task, but I will try. I cannot guarantee success though.' She stood up without saying goodbye to Selma and called the maid who escorted her to the main gate.

Loma stared at the wall of the house. 'Should I trust her?'

Minutes later as she sat in the taxi she hissed, 'I cannot trust her.'

Chapter Twenty-four

Short-term Memory

Time went past so quickly at Al-Jumeirah Beach. The tourists came in from the beach to the sandy desert hills in no time. There they went on adventures riding camels in the sand drag racing to get a boost of adrenalin to keep them going. Their evenings were spent at the shopping malls. Often, they took hours and hours to sift through the latest fashion and luxury products.

Culture seekers were interested in visiting the newly built village with architecture that resembled the old buildings of Dubai, when it had been a small port relying mainly on fishing. They could choose between the Irish pub and the theatre that put on international productions every now and then.

Zelfa sat in the pub sipping a pint of beer. She had missed the taste since she'd lived in Dubai. She came from a generation that thought a lady should drink wine not beer. In the United States the rules were different, and she enjoyed diverse beers there. She looked down at her body with disgust. Obesity — as a result of menopause. She liked to think that Jerry continued to love her, that all her appeal had not vanished. She was well aware of his escapades in the United States and Dubai, and she had confronted him with his credit card statement that showed a visit to an oriental massage parlour — a place famous for giving its clients happy endings. She'd discovered *that* when she looked up the massage parlour online. But why should she complain? Their sex life had come to an end a while ago. She wondered if Jerry had ever loved her or had he just married her as an act of chivalry. Or was it just that love did not last forever the same as everything in life.

The alcohol had messed with her head, and she was reliving the days when she lost her mother and had to grow up between two different countries and cultures. But she missed her homeland, Iraq, where she had spent the best days of her life. She had forgotten the horrible events and her suffering with her daughter. All of a sudden, a voice like thunder disturbed her nice memories.

'Darling, good to see you. Sorry, I am late. I had to work late.' Selma's voice brought back the worst of her memories — particularly the bad ones. She'd had to put up with her rudeness and cruelty after the death of her parents. Her older brother, Selma's husband, had inherited the family home. It was not a happy life for an orphan. Her brother was happy with his escape into alcohol, and it was left to Selma to run the home affairs in her own way. On the other hand, she had enjoyed a lavish life style and freedom with no restrictions as a young girl.

Zelfa wished Selma had not come. 'Not to worry, Selma. It is a different time in the East,' Zelfa said as she glanced into her brown beer.

'Well, it's okay for some. In this country, work regulations are in keeping with the western-world standards. Also, I am a very busy woman with my new job. Sorry, I should have cooked you a meal at my place.' Selma's words were half-hearted.

'Never mind. I've heard you have a good job.'

'What do you expect from a very knowledgeable, cultured and experienced woman like me?' Selma paused like an Aphrodite statue.

Zelfa knew she had never held down a job or finished any studies in her life, instead she gossiped and conspired to ruin others' lives.

'You know me, I am a straightforward person and I do not like to beat around the bush.' Selma changed the subject abruptly.

'I know you very well and it worries me. You are not transparent,' Zelfa said with apparent repulsion.

'Well, I try to help others and it is not my fault if people make foolish decisions,' Selma said with hostility.

'Okay, out with it. Am I part of a deal with Malaka? What are you up to?'

'To do the best for everyone, my dear.' Selma's voice was calm, which made Zelfa become even more concerned.

'So, you want me to spy on my husband. What do both of you want?'

'Calm down, dear, calm down. There is no harm that will come. I promise you. Your task is to help your native and adoptive countries alike.'

'I can see that Malaka has no plans to retire. If anything, she is upping her game. I do not want to be crushed as I have always been. I am stable and do not want to ruin my relationship with my husband.'

Selma took her smartphone from her Luis Vuitton handbag to unlock it. She handed it to Zelfa, who could not hide her shout of surprise.

'You see, my dear, men are pigs. They go wherever their underpants take them. He will not give a toss about your feelings when he chases cheap prostitutes. What a humiliating gesture.'

Zelfa threw the phone on the wooden table; it made a loud thud and drew the attention of the other clients.

'Listen to me, my dear. You cannot lose,' Selma said.

'What about Jerry, he will be upset if I betray him. I'll have no chance to get another partner. I am getting older.' Zelfa looked at her body and burst into tears.

'Do not worry. Men are like buses. They go and come. You only have to wait at the station. After all, you have the upper hand. Imagine if those photos get to his superiors; what would his fate be?' Selma lit her cigarette much to the bar tender's discomfort.

'What do I have to do?' Zelfa surrendered to her fate.

'Not to worry. Everything all in good time, my dear.' Her smoke spread up in the air much to the other customers' discomfort. The bar tender came close to asking her to quit smoking, but she sidetracked him. 'What are you waiting for? I want whiskey.'

'I think I need something even stronger,' Zelfa said. They both laughed loudly.

Selma was pleased with her triumph. She knew that Zelfa had succumbed.

Chapter Twenty-five

Contacts Everywhere

Malaka fanned herself with her Japanese silk fan and complained about the inefficiency of the air-conditioning system in Dubai Mall. It was easy to forget the endless days that the Iraqis suffered the summer heat without any air-conditioning following the recurrent power failures during the war. Winter was coming closer, and people were hoping for a fresh breeze to calm their nerves, having become fed up with living at the mercy of air-conditioning all year round. She would not admit it, but the fact that she was always hot could have been related to a menopausal hormonal disturbance rather than other factors.

She chose a small round table with two chairs squeezed into a corner of the cafe hidden from shoppers. Then she checked her mobile phone messages to ensure an important meeting would still take place. A broad smile covered her face when she was reassured that something positive would take place. She ate a chicken salad sandwich, then washed it down with a strong *cafe au lait*. Her patience was running out and to overcome her boredom and worries she ordered another coffee, followed by an expresso. She had always thought that French food was overrated. She believed that the small portions were tasteless, and she preferred heavy middle-eastern recipes. However, her inferiority complex and desire to climb the social ladder would not let her voice this openly because of her pride and lack of self-confidence.

Time was ticking by slowly before a young middle-eastern man with olive skin and a well-trimmed beard arrived wearing a Marks and Spencer blue suit, colour coordinated with a broad red tie that hid his bulging stomach. He spotted Malaka from a distance and approached her eager to start the conversation, yet he was out of breath. He must have been running. *How can a young man like him be that physically unfit?* Malaka wondered.

'I'm sorry. I was busy. Too much is going on at the embassy.' He made himself comfortable and sat on the chair opposite her.

'I'm sure you are busy, my dear; it is always the case,' she said with no enthusiasm, knowing it was not true.

'My superiors want to thank you for the recent recruits; we are very grateful to have new agents who are necessary in the hard times our country is going through. They are a valuable asset and will help us a great deal,' said as he sipped the milky coffee that he had ordered while he was rushing to the table. He made an annoying slurping noise as he sipped the hot drink in a hurry. Malaka looked at him with disgust. 'All my agents are gems,' she said.

'The recent information about the Americans' plans to withdraw from Iraq and hand it to the Iranians is very helpful,' he said with an anxious smile. Malaka smirked in triumph. 'I think it is time for us to rule by ourselves,' he said as he bit into a mille-feuille with messy cream filling. Malaka handed him a tissue to wipe his mouth.

'Now, let's talk business. I need the money transferred to my account by tonight.' Her stern tone was that of a relentless business woman or perhaps a harsh madam.

'Certainly, the Iraqi Government is grateful for your work.' His words were unclear as he ate the pastry with difficulty. She handed him a glass of water and gave him another look of disgust.

'We need more information from her or other agents to finish the task,' said in a quiet voice so curious ears wouldn't hear.

'In my profession, payment is in advance. You get what you pay, my dear. Rules are rules.' She giggled and he laughed. He had regained his confidence, which had been threatened by Malaka's strong personality and frank words.

'No problem, as an aside, can you arrange some girls for a very private night?' He came closer to her and began whispering to make sure no one else could hear. His voice was faint. This information was more secretive than any classified information.

'My dear, we can supply you with girls of all races and looks, and boys if you desire.' His mouth was drooling, not from the sweetness of the cake, but from lust about the coming night that he might share with his superiors. He took a bundle of US dollars from his jacket pocket. They were wrapped in a plastic bag. 'It's just a tip.' Malaka took it and watched this handsome, young man who could easily get any prostitute in Dubai, but he preferred the secrecy. Men often like to pay for a clandestine affair. She dialled a number while she watched him in a sadistic manner.

'Hello, I hope you are well. I hope so ... very important information ... but the pay is in advance.' She switched off her mobile and started tapping on the table while she was thinking.

I need to make a big box for those fools and leave this dangerous game soon.

Chapter Twenty-six

Back to the Office

The weather was getting milder by the day since winter had officially begun in the United Arab Emirates. This coincided with higher numbers of tourists coming from all over to enjoy the mild sunny weather, luxury hotels and excellent service, which they could not find in their native colder, more expensive countries. The locals and other work visitors who had deserted Dubai during the scorching hot summer months, had been enjoying the milder weather too.

Loma felt the urge to walk, the air-conditioning in private and public transport had given her recurrent headaches and sinusitis. She asked Hasna's car driver to stop before the end of her intended journey.

'Madam, shall I wait for you?' The Pathan Pakistani man dared to look directly into her eyes. She looked at his hazel eyes and his well-groomed beard with a lust that she suppressed. Her feelings towards men were long gone.

'No Ishtiaque, you go to the office. I will walk.' She looked into his eyes, which were full of desire. Intimacy would not happen between them.

Loma strolled on the beach, took a deep breath and thought about how her life had been turned upside down. The hotel beaches were crowded with westerners sunbathing in their swimsuits. She gazed at young western girls in bikinis. For her, those days were long gone. She remembered when she wore the bikini at the beach in Beirut and how she'd dared to do it again at the Alwiyah Club in the early 1970s. She sighed loudly and walked further until she reached the Sheikha's office at Sheikh Zayed Road. The doorman opened the door for her with a salute in keeping with her hierarchical position. Then he opened the lift door for her. She reached the third floor and a huge office which occupied the whole floor. The designer had made sure to marry the local cultural features with the Scandinavian-style furniture. Loma thought it was beautifully decorated. *Why do we rush to get the latest western designs? We have nice things of our own too.*

Before she opened her office door, the Asian porter spoke in broken Arabic. 'Ma'am a lady wants to talk to you.' Loma was taken by surprise. Hasna did not come to the office that early. As far as she knew, she was at the hospital attending to her ill grandson. She headed to her boss's office quickly, but the porter stopped her. 'No madam, it is the lady, Selma.' Loma lifted her eyebrows in astonishment. *Since when was Selma a lady?*

She had felt the need to have a fresh start with Selma after the recent reconciliation meet-up at Hasna's house. She slowed down as she marched towards her office. The porter knocked on the door and she heard a voice that was masterful and rehearsed when it said enter. Selma was wearing a blue suit because she would be attending a business meeting. Her dyed blonde hair was covered with colour-coordinated scarf. Her make-up was relatively modest.

'Hello, Loma, please come and sit down. How are you doing?' Selma said after the porter left. Loma was astonished at the kind angelic act that Selma was putting on, although it was not very convincing.

'Fine, I felt the need to walk this morning.' Loma decided to be pleasant to have a truce with her forever enemy, even if it was temporary.

'I see, that's why you are late.' Loma opted to ignore Selma's bossy comment. She wanted to have minimal conflict with Selma. She could not afford a confrontation to take place.

'Actually, I was watching people on the beach and thinking about our days at the Alwiyah Club in Baghdad. I remember you were one of the first who dared to wear Bikini in the 1960s.

I admired your courage.' Loma's words shocked Selma. She didn't know if they were a compliment or whether she was criticising her for being indecent according to religious and cultural tradition.

'Yes, I had a gorgeous figure, but I've always been conservative in my behaviour.' Selma wanted to put the matter right.

'What do you mean?' Loma asked.

'Nothing, my dear. We always need to remember the past because history repeats itself.'

Loma stood up abruptly and looked at Selma with disgust. She felt the need to smack her. Selma had a big smirk on her face.

'I better get on with work. We have a lot of preparations for the Iraqi refugees in Syria.' Loma left without knowing the reason Selma wanted to see her, apart from degrading her.

Selma ignored Loma's comment and picked up her phone as a sign of dismissal.

Loma left the office in her own world and ignored the porter who asked if she wanted to have tea in her office. *I want to live in a world without Selma. Is it my destiny or God's will to let her back into my life?* She knew for a fact that no reconciliation or working together was not possible with that woman.

Chapter Twenty-seven

Double Agent Work

Zelfa spent most of her spare time window shopping in the Dubai malls. It was an occupation that many of Dubai's residents engaged in. Her daily routine was synonymous with ladies having lunch. She enjoyed having coffee in a cafe with the expat community of both Iraqi and Americans and occasionally indulging in alcohol if the chance came. She had been to cinemas inside the mall, even alone at times. Jerry was more absent than present in her life. He always came up with excuses — travelling, meetings, work on so on. She coped with his indifference and was resigned to reality. She didn't want to confront him. She had decided to turn a blind eye to his extramarital affairs and bogus excuses for being away on *work trips*, whatever that meant despite the mounting evidence of his infidelity. She was fed up with finding lipstick marks on his shirts or phone numbers or obscure social media messages from unknowns with explicit sexual content.

Her only solace in life was her daughter, Sheza, who had settled after completing her studies at university and overcoming her alcohol and drug dependence. On the other hand, Zelfa had sleepless nights thinking that she might harm Jerry by passing information to Malaka. But did he care about her? And what were the consequences if she did not comply with Malaka's demands? Too many questions without answers gave her the urge to down a strong alcoholic beverage in the early hours of the afternoon to forget her dilemma.

Despite Jerry's disloyalty to her, she continued to have feelings for him. Her attachment to him was not only because she loved him dearly, but he had saved her by marrying her and enabling her to become a US citizen at a time when her country was in severe turmoil. She had to be more tolerant of his unfaithful behaviour. But there were limits and she was running out of patience. Her desire for revenge prevailed. Malaka had reassured her that the leaked information was for the good of Iraqi and the western population alike, to prevent further bloodshed in Iraq. She tried to believe this. Malaka continued to remind her about her husband's infidelity and the need to take action and save money before he threw her to the dogs. This was reinforced by Selma's ongoing nagging about how men were unpredictable. They *treat you like cheap meat, a bone that they will throw to the dogs.* Selma's broken record played in her mind. Should she believe them? She could not trust anyone. Zelfa asked herself these questions hundreds of times.

Today, she was meant to meet Selma at her flat in the Jumeirah district to have lunch while her nephew was at work. It was meant to be a confidential meeting, not even Ahmed was aware of it despite the difficulties Selma had hiding information from her son. Zelfa was a fool not to realise that Selma would report everything to him and maybe to others too. Nevertheless, Selma insisted on the meeting not taking place in a public place as per Malaka's instructions.

Both women hoped that Zelfa would obtain highly classified information from the US Embassy, which Malaka could pass to the Iraqis for the maximum benefit of all parties. She was more than a double agent. It was a win-win situation for Malaka, who was feeding all parties with information, in exchange for money and power. The visits in flats were the major method of contact with the odd ambiguous text messages so that they could communicate with pre-agreed terminology among the three of them.

Zelfa was looking at the sea from her balcony and refreshing herself with the light sea breeze, when the doorbell rang. The Asian maid rushed to open the door.

Selma came in wearing a long black *abaya* and addressed the maid in a rude voice.

'Where is your mistress?'

Zelfa came in a hurry to de-escalate the situation while Selma took off her *abaya* and showed off her cleavage in a tight T-shirt. Her Armani jeans were also tight and highlighted her fat aged body. As she handed the garment to the maid, she almost threw it at her in an aggressive disrespectful manner.

'Hello, dear.' Selma's voice was friendlier to Zelda than it had been to her maid.

'Hi, Selma,' Zelfa replied in a subdued voice.

'Are you okay?' Selma asked with fake warmth.

'Not really. I don't know where to start.' She felt the need to unburden herself by talking.

'Please tell me. I am not only your sister-in-law, but I am your older sister too. You grew up under my care.'

Zelfa often had flashbacks about Selma's harsh treatment of her after her parents passed away and she had to live with her helpless and hopeless brother. Selma's cruelty and rudeness were like something from a horror film. Zelfa identified with the character Cinderella.

'I am worried because of Malaka.' The name hit Selma's head like a rock. She composed herself and tried to be calm. 'Oh! Have you met her?'

'Yes. I have, thanks to you. I want to stop all these spying activities. I don't trust her. I'm worried about Jerry too.'

'Don't be silly; it's a minor thing. She said that it's all for the good of our country. No harm will come to Jerry,' Selma reassured her.

'Do you trust her?' Zelfa asked in a quiet voice.

Selma ran out of patience and opted to use a forceful threatening tone as plan B. 'Listen, you have already fallen into quicksand, and you have no option if you are to survive.'

'Is that a threat?' Zelfa was surprised by her change of tone.

'Darling, it's a big game, much bigger than us. You have to continue playing it to the end.'

Zelfa looked at the sea, wishing she could go there and disappear forever.

'And what are my options? Zelda's tone became more confident.

'What do you mean?' Selma was angry.

'What if I want to withdraw from the game.' Her voice was stronger and bolder as she asserted herself.

'It is a bigger game than you and me as I mentioned to you seconds ago. The dark forces have no mercy. We are mere pawns to them; we come and go. There is always a supply to replenish their needs if we disappear. There are thousands of Iraqis and even Americans who would beg to do this job. It's not the money but the self-importance, power and pride.' Selma's words made Zelfa think that becoming a US citizen was not enough to protect her from danger and injustice. 'Humans are the same everywhere,' she said more to herself.

Selma decided to open up because she could not keep it secret any longer. 'I have been approached by Malaka too and I had to cooperate with her despite my disgust at even talking to her, let alone working with her. But we have no other option, do we?' Selma's last statement stuck in Zelfa's head.' *It is the external question; does fate make us, or do we make our fate?'*

'Destiny is made for us, dear. It is even mentioned in the Quran,' Selma replied as if she had read her mind. Zelfa gave Selma a strange look. Did Selma have any consideration for anyone.

'Fine, where shall we start?' Zelfa asked her sister-in-law.

'Dead easy, try to get information from his paperwork. Any documents will do.'

'Well, it's not a big task if I dismiss the morality side of it.'

Chapter Twenty-eight

Summer Break in Marbella

Time passed so quickly. Summer was back again. Selma had started to complain about the heat. Winter had been a short honeymoon from the hot weather in UAE. The temperature had risen dramatically to forty something with suffocating humidity that was pushed from the Gulf to inland. The mass exodus of the locals and residents had begun as they fled to cooler places in other parts of the world.

Sheikha Hasna's home and office staff were running like bees to organise a temporary move to a cooler place. She was in the habit of spending the summer at her villa in Marbella in Spain. It was a popular place for wealthy middle-eastern tourists since it had been discovered by the Saudi monarchy. They had enjoyed its weather and similarity of setting to middle-eastern cities and even some traditions since the time it was discovered in the 1970s and 1980s. Since then, the area between Puerta Banús and the town centre, luxurious villas had been occupied by the rich and famous with a significant representation from middle-eastern rich and famous personalities.

Hasna was no different from the rest. The villa had been gifted to her by her late husband and she continued the tradition of spending summers there with her family but more often alone since the death of her husband and once her children had grown up and fled the maternal nest. She was a regular frequenter of this attractive spot in the world with her routine of annual visits in summer. The only time she didn't go there was in the case of an emergency such as the birth of one of her grand-children or spending the month of Ramadan in her native country, if it happened to be in the summer.

Hasna entered the office with her mini entourage and called in Loma and Selma.

'*Al salamu alaykum*,' Hasna started the conversation with a strict professional face while the two women looked at her with the obedience of good girls to their mother or their strict headmistress. They were competing for the most complimentary response.

'I hope you've sorted out the differences between you,' she said with confidence believing that she had fixed the case well. They looked at each other with equally reciprocated feelings and thoughts — *I hate her guts. I cannot stand her breath any closer to me, I wish she was dead.*

'We are fine Ma'am,' they said like schoolgirls wanting to impress their teacher.

'We are old friends.' They did not mean a word of it.

'Good. That what I like to hear.' She took the headmistress's position. 'We need to prepare for my summer trip.'

'Which trip?' asked Selma.

'Oh, sorry. Loma knows. I spend summer in Marbella, but I don't want our charity work to cease while we are living the high life. Thus, you are going to accompany me on this trip.'

The women were gobsmacked with surprise. They have not been on a holiday abroad since the embargo on Iraq during the 1990s and after the United States led invasion in the early 2000s because of the travel ban imposed on Iraqis who could not get visa to a Western country. Western countries refused to issue Iraqis visas.

Before they uttered a word, Hasna stopped them. 'You know, I will sort out your travel arrangements to get you a Schengen visa, so you can enter Spain as tourists with no problems whatsoever.' She looked at their faces with a mix of surprise and disbelief that made her feel powerful. 'Please make sure to facilitate everything so you can continue working from Marbella,' she added. When the phone rang, Hasna indicated the importance of the call and ushered the women out with a gentle hand. Loma and Selma left. They shut the door behind them and looked at each other. They smiled in unison with a sign of agreement for the first time ever. 'Hooray!' They both cheered before they rushed to their mobile phones to let their nearest and dearest know about the happy event. At long last they felt the need to have a truce or a break from their long-lived conflict. It was a reciprocal understanding between them for the first time ever. It seemed that Hasna was wiser than they thought or was it just a rest in the war between them? Time would tell.

Chapter Twenty-nine

Time in Marbella

The next few weeks were like a dream for Selma and Loma. They had not had the taste or the buzz of travel since the invasion of Iraq in 1990. And even worse for Selma, she could not move abroad during the Iraq-Iran war during the 1980s when Saddam banned travel for the population to stop the exodus of men fleeing a relentless war. The only exemptions were those who worked for the government, such as Loma, who enjoyed travelling freely much to the envy of Selma.

The travel preparations was going ahead. The tickets were booked to travel straight from Dubai to Malaga Airport with Emirates Airlines, which was popular in the summer months of that year. Selma and Loma met at Dubai International Airport and for the first time they had a friendly conversation to reassure each other. They exchanged kisses briefly to prove their reconciliation in front of Hasna. They were surprised by the VIP treatment they received from customs and immigration staff. It was thanks to Hasna, of course. They felt anxious having to travel ahead of Hasna, who was meant to visit her grandson who was receiving treatment at a London hospital.

The women enjoyed the trip on the plane with a special treatment they were not used to, especially Selma. Whereas Loma re-lived her past days of affluence. They were friendly to each other during the flight. Selma took the opportunity to show her dominant character to the air hostesses by complaining about anything and everything. Loma tried to ignore her and was happy with the unofficial truce between them.

They reached Malaga Airport, which they found cute. A car with a Moroccan chauffeur was waiting for them and they were greeted in Arabic and then driven to Marbella, an hour's drive in heavy summer traffic. The women kept silent on the route to the city. They were distracted by the scenery with childlike excitement.

As they drove through the outskirts of Marbella to reach the centre, the road was lined with grand villas built in a mixture of Moorish and European styles. The car reached Puerta Banús, which had villas that were even more grand.

Hasna's villa was painted sunset yellow to reflect off the heat. The entrance was huge but more modest than her mansion in Dubai. The entrance was bright white, and the walls were adorned with photos of Marbella. The villa had five bedrooms. The master had an ensuite and there was a bathroom shared by the other bedrooms. The servants occupied an annex. Two huge reception rooms were decorated in middle-eastern design combined with Spanish. Hasna had made sure to include pictures of the local environs and a depiction the history of the area as a fishing village before it became a famous resort when it was discovered by European royalty after the second world war and the middle-eastern oil boom. Mass tourism then followed from all over the world.

A North African chef was employed during the summer months to cook middle-eastern recipes, predominately seafood that were served on the terrace overlooking the sea. Seafood was readily available and Hasna made it a priority that his cooking skills included Gulf-style cuisine and the local cuisine. She made sure he had a big variety of ingredients available. She remembered vividly how they struggled to secure camel meat and milk during her late father-in-law's visits to Marbella in the 1980s. She had told Loma about this when they caught up for a meal at Hasna's place. How they could not source essential Bedouin food. Her father-in-law had wanted to continue his ancestor's lifestyle. Before Hasna became a widow, at a reasonably young age, she used to put on banquets at her villa for all Emirates and other Gulf State dignitaries when they spent summer in Marbella.

Selma's excitement to travel after all those years took over, and she decided to temporarily give up her feud with Loma in the weeks prior to their trip. She felt she had to comply with Hasna's planned truce, for the moment at least.

'I cannot believe you are travelling with that slut,' Ahmed said prior to her departure.

'Sometimes, you have to bend with the wind, dear, to get to your goals,' Selma replied.

When Hasna arrived in Marbella, she was happy to believe that she had sorted out the two strong personalities and made peace between them. Although she did not know the root cause of their conflict, or that they continued to suffer.

Shopping trips to local malls and exclusive boutiques that catered for the rich and famous, to buy appropriate clothing for Hasna and themselves were an ongoing business. Hasna extended her generosity and paid for some of their shopping, which was heaven for both of them. On the occasion that Selma went to the shops by herself her eyes wandered over the shop windows and settled on a window full of swimming clothes. *That bikini is a dream, I used to wear ones like that in my twenties in Baghdad and abroad. I looked so good, back then.* But she couldn't wear a bikini in the years that followed the western invasion to Iraq.

In a small cafe in downtown Marbella, Loma went over her past when she'd felt the need to get away from her son's house and her need to have a break. Her daughter-in-law had been over the moon to have free time with her family without Loma. *If only I didn't have to put up with that bitch, Selma. She is threatening me with my big secret, and I could lose all the privileges I have obtained from Hasna's friendship.* The excitement and the discovery of the unknown and the vital need for survival made the reconciliation carry on for the time being.

Selma brought copies of Emirati *Zahrat Al Khaleej* and the Kuwaiti *Osrati* and other women's magazines to look at the latest fashions for clothes and make-up. She struggled to read the English, let alone the

Spanish and she hoped to find some Arabic magazines at the local book stores.

Their dreams had come true. They enjoyed meals on the terrace cooked by a talented chef who flew from Madrid to help. Hasna held her place in upper society when she spent time in Marbella. She continued to maintain her serious facade along with her sense of duty as she continued working for the charities, much to the women's dismay. It was business as usual. In the mornings there were emails to read and phone calls to UAE and other parts of the world.

Afternoons were for lunch and relaxing, perhaps a siesta or even a walk on the beach or escape to a local cafe. Evenings were devoted to shopping or eating out.

Selma wanted to go out and mingle with others and to eat and drink, which was banned at the villa. There were strict rules about which restaurants they could eat in, and the meat had to be strictly *halal* and, of course, no pork.

They gazed with temptation at the swimming pool, not daring to wear swimming costumes in front of Hasna. Their thoughts constantly went back to the good old days. Nevertheless, they decided to enjoy some pleasures including the weather, the scenery and the food.

When Selma and Loma couldn't take their eyes off the muscular body of a flirtatious Spanish waiter food was not their only pleasure. They giggled.

One morning after Hasna took a phone call, they heard her talking louder than usual in Arabic. They rushed across the marble-paved lounge overlooking the sea and stood by her bedroom. They were ready to rescue her if necessary. The waited behind the closed door and tried to pick up words and ascertain information that could help them to offer help or serve their mistress. Servants were lined up behind Selma and Loma. They were trying to eavesdrop. Hasna stopped speaking and her footsteps on the marble floor were loud. She was angry and worried. Loma and Selma dashed to the living room in an attempt not to be seen being nosy and unnecessarily curious about their mistress, even though they were concerned.

'Loma, Selma, please come,' Hasna shouted. Her voice came from the doorway of her bedroom. She knew they'd been listening. They hoped that she would consider them concerned about her rather than nosy. The women went cautiously through the door like two loyal dogs.

'I must leave for Dubai, today,' Hasna shouted and burst into tears.

'Why, your highness?' Selma asked in a sheepish voice.

'My grandson, Abed, has been admitted to the hospital again with more health complications.' She was hysterical and hugged Loma much to Selma's evident envy.

'You know he suffers from physical health problems compounded with learning difficulties,' she said as she sobbed.

'He was fine when you visited him in London,' Loma said.

'He has been well and managed to get back home where he's made some progress with his physical health at least, but things have gone wrong.' Selma rushed to her with the tissue box and tried to wipe Hasna's tears, but the latter took the tissue herself.

'I must leave soon. Please call the travel agent to book the first available flight.'

Selma approached Hasna a few minutes later. 'I have done it.'

Hasna thanked her half-heartedly but continued to cling to Loma's chest. Selma felt humiliation as if she was a second-rate person.

I wish you both harm. 'We are at your service, Ma'am, shall we pack our belongings now?' asked Selma.

'No, no need, you can continue to work from here. It is not fair to spoil the break that you longed for, for ages.'

The villa was a hive of busy bees as Hasna's clothes and belongings, which were small in comparison to her bigger wardrobe in her house in Dubai, were packed.

The flight was booked via Madrid, but the agent managed to get her a business class seat on the first Emirates plane out of Malaga. The travel agent was Moroccan and made a huge fuss about how hard he had worked to get a seat on a fully booked flight. As he'd hoped he was given a generous tip by Hasna.

When the VIP Mercedes arrived to take Hasna to the airport, Selma and Loma were in competition to carry her luggage, much to the dismay of the servants and the chauffeur who were eager for handsome tips.

Hasna ushered the women away with her hand. 'Ladies, there is no need to accompany me. I want to speak to my lazy daughter-in-law for neglecting her children and it is not nice to humiliate her in front of others.' They waved her goodbye and looked at each other with raised eyebrows. As they watched the car disappearing down the driveway, they finally spoke.

'Freedom at last,' they said in unison. They faced each other and looked into each other's eyes as they had not done for a long time. They giggled like school children.

Chapter Thirty

Adios Freedom

In Marbella, every day was like the next. The villa was full of tranquility, unlike the buzz in central Dubai.

Selma and Loma followed the same routine each day of having a meal together, if they were in good moods. Phone calls with Hasna had diminished as her contact and interest in work faded. Her grandson was on the mend, and she was spending most of her time at his bedside in the hospital rehabilitation centre close to her home where she insisted on nursing him by herself. Her work ethic had lapsed for the time being. Perhaps the near miss of losing her grandson had made her review her priorities. Family came first according to her preaching.

Meanwhile Loma and Selma were roaming freely in Marbella with no constraints, not only were they visiting cafes, shops and restaurants, but they had their own agendas. Selma was back to her old self and living life to the full, having missed out for the last few years and Loma was the same. They had to work together, but the mistrust between the two would always be a problem even though they had called a temporary truce.

On a typical day, they would have a meal or two together, either at home or at one of the local restaurants. The meals started out friendly but invariably ended up with disagreements and hostile confrontations. They watched each other closely.

One afternoon when there was a fresh breeze from the sea and temperature was in the late twenties or early thirties, which was very mild in comparison to the scorching heat of the Gulf, tourists had come from all over the northern parts of Europe for a small dose of sun. Men and women were semi-comatose on loungers all over the Playa del Alicate at Los Monteros. Selma was wearing her blue bikini, sunbathing and flirting with a handsome young waiter, and sipping cocktails, which made her tipsy in no time because she hadn't touched alcohol for ages. She tried to read some of the Arabic magazines she'd brought from the villa with not much success. She attempted to plunge into the sea, but the water was too cold. *It would be warmer in Dubai, but there was no way I would dare to swim there.* She was enjoying the sun and the refreshing breeze, when she heard a voice. 'Well Selma, you are having a good time, aren't you?' She turned to the source of the voice. *Ugly voice, that ruins good looks and beauty,* she thought of Loma. She was wearing a T-shirt that covered her long shorts; both were covered by an *abaya*.

'What are you doing here?' Selma asked.

'The same as what you are doing, dear, only I'm a bit more decent,' Loma replied with a giggle.

'Listen! You like it, actually we both do,' Selma replied.

'Indeed. It is the one thing we agree on, but it should stay secret between us. If Hasna came to learn about what we are doing, it would be the end of us.'

'Yes, we would be expelled from paradise,' Selma said. They giggled.

'Take it easy and show your bikini,' Selma added.

'How do you know I'm wearing a bikini?' Loma asked.

'I can guess from the way your breasts are bulging from your T-shirt.' Her expert eyes never failed her. Loma took of her T-shirt with hesitation. She was embarrassed to show her breasts covered only by a bikini top. As a Muslim woman she felt guilty exposing parts of her body, but she braved it.

'Oh no! Your boobs are bit saggy,' Selma said and laughed.

'Look at your tummy; I thought you were pregnant,' Loma replied. Before their conversation culminated into a fight, Selma accosted the waiter in heavily accented English and ordered two sangrias. The drink would pacify the situation.

The young, olive-skinned waiter came with two glasses of sangria. Selma looked at him and sent him a light air kiss full of lust after many years of deprivation and lack of physical intimacy. He returned the kiss with a smile that showed his white teeth in contrast to his dark beard and moustache. 'Bella,' he said in the Italian way. She could not resist the Latino charm.

'You've still got it.' Loma turned her head away from Selma to hide her envious smile. 'You've still got it,' she repeated.

'Of course, darling, and you too.' Selma's statement was half-hearted and reminded her of Selma's old comments about how her face looked like a cow ... according to a mutual friend. They had exchanged inflammatory statements in the past. They both enjoyed these moments.

Selma raised her sangria and looked into Loma's eyes. 'Let's have fun as long as the wicked witch is not here.'

'You mean, Hasna. She's a nice lady,' Loma replied.

'We are mere servants to her. Do not forget your higher status than hers.'

'I think you have a point. I helped her a great deal when she was struggling to get used to London life when our husbands worked in the embassies back then.' Loma felt the guilt of betraying her friend and the fear of Selma's well-known slanders. But she could not hide her minor grudge against her best friend and her feeling of inferiority.

'By the way, any news about that husband of yours?' Selma asked.

'Nothing. We are concerned about his fate.' Loma tried not to show concern.

'I bet, although he would not care about you.'

'I think you are right.' Selma was on a mission to breakdown Loma's defences by hitting a raw wound hard.

When the handsome young waiter came closer to serve customers lying under the parasol next to them, he winked and smiled.

'I wouldn't mind some time with him,' Selma said with a laugh that was reciprocated by Loma.

'Why not,' said Loma. They laughed loudly and clinked their glasses. '*Sahtak, santé, cheers, salute*,' they said in all the languages they knew.

Chapter thirty-one

Turn of Fate

The holiday was over and like all summer holidays it ended with pleasant memories from the past. The happy ones would stay forever, and the bad ones would be forgotten. What happened in Marbella stayed in Marbella. Life was back to normal. And it was no different for Selma and Loma. The old feud could never die between them. The fact that they were together more often, the more the truce conditions were ignored. Hasna was busier than ever with her family and the management of the office was left to the two rivals who were striving for power and control. Back stabbing and argument were no different to that of the pre-holiday honeymoon, if not worse. The charity work progress was sluggish, and the office staff were fed up with the ever-changing decisions. The staff were torn between the two. They didn't know which side to take.

One morning, Selma arrived at the office early in contrast to her usual late attendance. She asked the porter to make her a cup of coffee using her usual rude tone, which he tolerated so he could keep his job and feed his family back home. She thought that he had mastered making the Arabic coffee better than any Bedouin man and she was addicted to it. Even so, she never uttered a word of gratitude or thanks. He brought the coffee with a bundle of Arabic newspapers. Selma had taken over Hasna's secretary, Marwa, and she asked her if Loma had arrived.

'No, Ma'am,' the secretary replied in her distinct Syrian accent.

Selma started turning the pages of a newspaper as she sipped her bitter coffee. Then all of a sudden, she choked on her coffee and sprayed it over the newspaper. She stared at the headline: *Iraqi Lady Strangled in her Flat in Central Duba*i. She could not focus on the details, and she tried hard to collect her thoughts. *Am I dreaming?* She went over and over the details to pick up the name of the victim. She started to read in a high-pitched voice. The name was Malaka Mahmood. The name gave her the shivers. Her hands were shaking. She felt the urgent need to shout or at least to voice her horror at the news. She threw the newspaper to the ground. Her shaking hands struggled to find her mobile phone. It took a while to retrieve Zelfa's number from the contacts' list, but she found it after a few attempts. The phone rang then went to an answering machine. *Why doesn't she answer?* Selma ran out of patience. The second call went to the answering machine. Selma could hardly wait for the machine to start recording. She left a disjointed message quickly with muddled words.

'Zelfa are you okay? Let me know.' Selma ended the call and walked to the door.

She was confused, but felt she needed protection from something unknown. She felt danger was looming and coming her way. Just then someone knocked on her door.

'What do you want? Selma said in an aggressive voice that was not her normal one. The porter opened the door with hesitation. He knew how aggressive and rude Selma could be.

'Ma'am, Lady Loma wants to see you.'

'I have no time for her.' Selma slammed the door in the poor man's face.

Minutes later, the porter opened the door with extreme care and Loma entered with confident steps. She was wearing a blue jacket with a colour-coordinated shorter than usual skirt. 'Did you want me, Selma?'

Selma could not utter a word. Her mouth muscles were too paralysed to move. She pointed at the newspaper.

Loma took a step back and bent to pick it up. 'Oh no! I don't believe it,' she shouted. With unsteady steps she staggered to a chair and dropped into it. 'Was she working as a madam here?'

Selma glanced with an evil look at Loma. 'There is no point in slagging off the dead.'

'You must know her better than I did,' Loma said.

'What do you mean?'

'You have befriended her since her feet touched this country.'

Selma pulled open the drawer of the mahogany chest to get her cigarettes. Loma stared with astonishment to see her smoking inside a building against the regulations.

'We need to be careful. I must be candid with you, Hasna liked Malaka when they met at the concert. She will be upset. But she is clueless as to her past and to yours,' Loma added.

Selma puffed her smoke from her mouth. 'And to yours too dear. Hasna does not know how to choose her friends.'

'What do you mean? Malaka was your friend, and you were both up to something. Do you think I hadn't noticed your manoeuvres to get Malaka close to Hasna. What were you up to?' Loma's voice was raised, and Selma pushed her body back against the chair.

'Nothing, you think that you can monopolise people. I know how selfish you can be. You want to grab all the benefits for yourself.'

'Hasna is my old dear friend. I knew her from the days our husbands worked in London in the 1980s. I will protect her from you at any price.'

Selma released a loud hysterical laugh. 'Oh dear, oh dear. You are the guardian angel who wants to shield her friends. My advice to you, is to try to cover up your past. Imagine if Hasna knew you were a tart, a bed hopper who lost her virginity and covered it by cheating on her husband with an operation to mend her purity. Just think.' Selma poured out her venom with relief.

Loma's breathing accelerated like a steam engine as she came towards Selma at full speed. Selma could not stand up and lost her balance. Loma grabbed her neck and tried to strangle her.

'You are killing me,' Selma said in a suffocating voice between intermittent coughs.

'Then I will save the world from your evil,' Loma shouted. The noise attracted the attention of the other employees who dashed in to free Selma from Loma's strong hands.

'Call the police, she's mad. She needs to go to a mental institution. She will kill me. She's mad.'

Selma deliberately threw her body onto the cold marble floor in a histrionic way like a diva in a major film role or an opera production. She turned her back to the others and pretended to fix her dress while she tore the front to make it look as if she had been assaulted by Loma.

The young secretary was confused and didn't know what to do. She looked at the others and waited for instructions.

'What are you waiting for, call the police,' shouted Selma.

The young woman became even more confused.

'What a low-life you are. I never touched you,' Loma shouted to the surprise of the staff. She never raised her voice — ever.

'If you don't have anything to fear, then you should not be worried,' Selma challenged her in front of the group.

'Okay then, suit yourself.' Loma left the room in a hurry.

Selma turned to the young secretary. 'What are you waiting for? Call the police?' she shouted.

The young woman dialled the number on the landline. 'Allo, police? Please come to this address. It's an emergency.'

Selma raised herself with a fit and strong move and pushed away the many hands that came to her aid. Much to the staff's surprise, she rushed to her smartphone, took photos of her torn dress and contorted her face as if she was in pain.

Loma was dazed; she didn't know what to say or do. 'What an amazing actor. She could have won an oscar,' Loma said, but everyone ignored her. She turned her head. The office staff marched towards Selma, surrounded her and showered her with words of concern as they thanked Allah that she was safe. Loma picked up Selma's smirk through the mass of people — police and first aid included.

Chapter Thirty-two

When the Dust Settles

Filipino nurses rushed around the VIP patient in the private psychiatric hospital in Dubai. The senior psychiatrist hurried from his home after receiving a phone call saying he needed to see a very special patient. The hospital staff ignored many of the other patients. Word had spread that Sheikha Hasna had called to make sure her best friend or her *sister* as she called her, while talking to the manager of the hospital, was okay.

Loma sat in a room in a semi-comatose state. She had been given a lorazepam injection. It was as if she was drunk from drinking an excess of alcohol. The strong tranquilizer she'd been given was only used in emergencies because it was addictive. She responded to the nurses with slurred speech.

The psychiatrist arrived in a hurry, he had not finished buttoning up his shirt and the nurses giggled about his protruding stomach.

'Ma'am, I hope you are well,' the nurse asked Loma in heavily accented English with a south-east Asian accent. Loma found it difficult to articulate her response. She sent a look of innocence at the young nurse, which implied she didn't know what had happened or why she had ended up where she was. The group gathered nearby wearing white coats added to her confusion.

'You are in the hospital. It is stress, that is all. We will escort you home and a nurse will accompany you and stay with you overnight.'

'What sort of hospital is this?' Loma asked.

'A mental health institution,' the nurse said and then she rushed to comfort Loma when she saw the horror on her face that it was a mental health institution.

At that moment the psychiatrist came in. The name of Sheikha Hasna was prized. Her support of the charity attached to the hospital was vital. He was full of gratitude and wished to elevate himself in Hasna's eyes.

'I am fine, doctor. I'm staying with my son and his family. Please, keep this a secret. I do not want my family to know what happened,' Loma said.

'Ma'am, we are bound by a strict confidentiality code,' he said as he wrote a prescription that included antidepressants and anti-anxiety medication. His Iraqi Arabic accent made her feel concerned and paranoid. What if the news about her spread among the Iraqi ex-pat community. She wanted to get greater confirmation from the psychiatrist about the confidentiality. But she knew Selma would do the job. Her main aim was to tarnish Loma's image before everyone, and in particular Hasna and the Iraqi ex-pat community.

The porter took the prescription, saluted the doctor and rushed to the pharmacy.

'Please say if anything is bothering you or giving you any kind of stress,' the doctor said as he tried to get more information to identify what had triggered her breakdown.

She looked at his salt and pepper hair and goatee beard and wondered if she could trust a stranger with her secret. According to the saying, there were no secrets in the East. At least not for those associated with the local community.

'It seemed that you were stressed out at work and the staff called the ambulance,' he added.

Loma's recollection of what had occurred was vague. She tried to remember. The office. Selma on the floor. The police. It was all vague. It was then that her mobile rang. She glanced at the screen and saw Hasna's name. She felt ashamed and did not want to reveal the reason behind her breakdown. But could she tell the truth? She was convinced that the truth would destroy their friendship. She pressed the green icon with a trembling hand.

'Loma, where are you? I am dead worried about you'. Hasna's voice was full of concern.

'I am fine; please do not worry. I was under immense pressure. I'm sorry.' Loma burst into tears.

'I tried to explain to Selma that your reaction was out of the norm. You must be worried about the news of your husband,' Hasna said.

Why did Hasna say that? Was she making excuses for her? Loma had almost forgotten about him. She might be concerned about the father of her boys. That was all. And she wanted to avoid discussing him. 'To be honest, I can't remember much about what happened,' Loma replied.

Hasna went quiet. There was a pause before she spoke again. 'I was told that you lost it and hit Selma. I know she can be difficult, but she is not a bad person. She has forgiven you and is willing to start afresh with you.'

Loma's memory returned. Selma had come to accuse her of being the main suspect in Malaka's death. The discussion had escalated to an argument when Selma threatened to disclose Loma's secret past. The argument escalated to a physical confrontation. She recalled hazy visions of police and paramedics. She understood what the psychiatrist said about the dissociative state she went through which could be a product of stress. Malaka's murder had had its effect on her fragile psyche; so too had Selma's threats.

'Listen, take some time off. If you want to have a break, please do. My villa in Marbella is at your disposal any time you want to go there. I will pop in and see you at home soon,' Hasna added before she ended the call.

Loma could not understand why Hasna was referring to her ex-husband. He was history to her. She grabbed her smartphone and began searching under, Riaz Adil, ex-minister in the Iraqi regime. She found out that he had been captured by the US military and there was an ongoing trial led by the newly appointed Iraqi Government. To her relief, he was cleared of criminal activity, but he had been imprisoned for an indefinite time. She thought about her two boys and the effect on their mental health and their future. *I hope that's the end of it. At least Riaz was helpful in diverting attention away from my current mess with Selma.*

Just then the nurse approached her with medication and the psychiatrist started to explain the dosage. She was absentminded and didn't register a word. She covered her hair with a scarf and put the medication into her Gucci handbag. *I think I need a plan to sort out Selma, more than medication. Although I might need the medication to have clear thinking. Selma cannot get away with this anymore.*

The psychiatrist had mentioned talking therapy or counselling and said it was important to sort out what had triggered the breakdown. But she felt that she did not need his services.

She followed the nurse to the car waiting outside the hospital. She tried to keep up with the young nurse's steps, but the medication slowed her down, even so, her thoughts of revenge were simmering in the forefront of her mind.

Chapter Thirty-three

The Others' Secrets

Winter was coming to an end. The weather was getting warmer, so people were moving from the cool outdoor life to another hibernation from the heat in the air-conditioned world.

Hasna's charity office was as busy as ever because of more problems all over the world. War in the Middle East was ongoing. Refugees and destitute people, mostly women and children needed the help of good-willed people like Hasna to alleviate a small fraction of their misery.

Loma was back in the office. She tried to avoid Selma as much as she could to avert any unnecessary confrontation. The altercation had been hinted at in the State-controlled tabloid press. Hasna's increased presence in the office had calmed down the tense atmosphere between the two women.

Loma had noticed that Selma had been disappearing more frequently from the office. This was unusual for someone who had been glued to her office chair. To begin with, she thought that Selma was keeping a low profile and had become a pacifist. *That is not in her genes.* Then she had another thought. She had learnt the need to be ready to attack Selma at any time. She could not stop speculating about what would happen in the second round.

The investigation regarding Malaka's murder had been deliberately buried in the sand. Rumours spread among the expat Iraqi community that she had been murdered by the CIA, Iraqi Intelligence or even VIP politicians because she had supplied them with prostitutes. It seemed that there was not much sympathy about her death from the public. After all, she was a pimp with a history of being a prostitute.

Loma wanted to find out information about Selma's movements. She knew that Selma's social circle had tightened up since Malaka's murder. The case had been closed after investigation showed that Selma had been involved. Zelfa had been forced to return to the United States.

The slogan "know your enemy", was Loma's mantra to ensure her safety and survival.

Selma was a bomb waiting to explode. And there was no doubt that she was the enemy who was keeping away while the dust settled.

From the reports she obtained from the staff and the porter who manned her flat, Loma noticed that Selma's disappearances had a pattern. They tended to occur on Sundays. Sundays were a working day in the Emirates, whereas Fridays and Saturdays were the weekend. Hasna was keen for her Muslim staff to have Fridays off, in case they wanted to go to Friday prayers. Christian staff were allowed to be absent on Sundays, if they wished to attend mass at church.

Loma also noticed that Selma was getting closer to certain staff, and she had become more arrogant and was looking down upon others who she thought were below her professional and social echelon.

Loma took notice of Rana, a young Indian young woman from Goa. She was a quiet girl who kept to herself. Loma knew that she was a well-disciplined polite person who Selma used to ignore. Selma used to take the mickey out of her and bully the young girl. What made Loma suspicious was the disappearance of both Rana and Selma on Sundays. She also noticed the sudden care and attention that came from Selma towards the quiet clerk. She even proposed promoting her with a salary rise. Rana started to spend longer than usual time in Selma's office too. Loma was aware that Rana was a practising Catholic and attended Sunday mass regularly. She realised that the starting point to uncover what Selma was up to must begin with Rana.

It's a bit fishy; I must find out what is taking place, Loma thought when she discovered the disappearance of the two at the same time.

After a few hours of waiting and deliberation, she called Rana into her office.

Rana was nervous when entered the office. She was afraid of losing her job. She had financially dependent family members in India, who waited for her monthly money to arrive so they could live off it.

Loma started the conversation by asking how her work was going and if she was settled in her job. Then she asked her about her family. The questions made Rana shake with fear. She was worried that she had made a mistake or not completed certain tasks efficiently enough. She knew that Loma did not care about her and that she must have had an agenda.

After a short pause, which gave Rana the shivers, Loma carried on. 'I am happy with your work, and I want to make sure that no one bothers or bullies you.'

'No, Ma'am, everyone is kind to me,' the young girl replied with hesitation.

'I am worried that Selma might be harassing you.'

'No, Ma'am. Selma is the boss and I listen to her.'

'You know I am her boss. And I have a duty to protect you.' Loma raised her voice because she had failed to extract any information from the terrified girl.

'I will keep that in mind,' replied the girl before Loma told her she could leave. *I think the key to Selma's movements is to monitor this young girl. There is something she is hiding. I smell a rat.* Loma logged in to her top-desk computer and accessed the Internet. She typed Private Detective into the search engine. A list of the newly formed companies appeared on the screen. Loma spent some time going through them and reading the reviews. Then she picked her mobile and dialled.

'Allo, I am interested in using your services,' she said.

Chapter Thirty-four

Summer is Coming

The locals were planning where to spend at least part of summer in cooler places in the world. The first choice was Europe. The travel itch had reached its peak. The charity office had become quieter as staff numbers were dropping day by day. Loma and Selma's last adventure in Marbella gave them both a feeling of nostalgia, but going there again was impossible after the recent events.

Then came the day when Selma knocked on Loma's office and entered before being granted permission.

'Hello, dear, how are you?' Selma said in an unusual over-friendly tone of voice. Loma sensed that Selma was up to something.

'I'm fine, thanks. How is your son? Is he happy at his work?' Loma tried to smooth the atmosphere by becoming friendlier despite her apparent dislike of Selma.

Selma's suspicious nature made her worry that Loma might harm her or her son. She could distinguish between the genuine and false warmth from her rival who was now her enemy. She started to complain about the pay and bad treatment, partly to distract Loma's focus on her and to protect herself from envy by not showing off her prosperity. Selma recited verses from Quran to expel evil spirits.

'I wish him the best and *mashallah*, he will succeed in a better job,' Loma said after noticing the change in her.

'I wish your family the best. How is your daughter-in-law? She seems to be a difficult woman.'

Loma knew that Selma was aiming to hurt her by commenting on her daughter-in-law. She knew Selma's tactics of extracting and twisting information from others and passing it on and causing rifts between people. It was no secret that Loma did not get on well with her daughter-in-law, but she would never give Selma the chance to gloat about it. She ignored her comment.

'We are fine,' she said to close the subject.

'Where are you going to spend the summer?' Selma started a new discussion after failing to irritate Loma with her comment about her daughter-in-law.

'Actually, I have a niece who lives in Canada, and she is asking me to visit her. I have not seen her for ten years.'

'Can you get a visa on your Iraqi passport in view of your affiliation to the old Iraqi regime?' Selma's response was full of venom.

'My husband has been cleared from war crimes as you are well aware.' Loma's voice was full of emotion. She wanted to slap Selma but decided to put up with her aggravation and not be upset by her.

'Well, regardless, he has been imprisoned by the new regime.' Selma uttered her words with the contented tone of a winner.

'Hasna will sponsor me to obtain a Canadian tourist visa. What about you, are you going somewhere?'

'No, I'm staying here. I will put up with the heat.' Selma was brimming with anger and jealousy.

'Hasna is not going away to Marbella or elsewhere. She wants to hang around her extended family in the Emirates.' Loma wanted to confirm her closer position to the boss.

'I wanted to clear the air between us, Loma. We are in the same trench.' Her attempt to show repentance did not dent Loma's defences.

'Life is too short to waste it on such insignificant differences,' Loma replied. Their eyes met in search of the truth which genuinely they could not find. The only thing they had in common was their desire for survival for the fittest. It was a jungle. Selma stood up to leave and tried not to pull a face of disgust while Loma pretended to check her emails. She opened her account eagerly hoping for a report from the detective agency. It was composed in Arabic and full of grammatical errors. After she read it, Loma smirked and looked through the window at the endless sea that she wished would wash away all her stresses.

'At last, Selma. I've got you at last.' She switched off her mobile and dialled the travel agency.

'Please book a return ticket to Toronto,' she said to the agent.

Chapter Thirty-five

The Canadian Adventure

The Emirates airbus flight landed at Pearson Airport in Toronto. The passengers were of predominately middle-eastern and Asian origin. The majority had been granted immigration status either as investors or refugees. They had tried to exchange their lucrative, well-paid jobs in the Emirates to secure residency in Canada which had opened its door to immigrants to boost its declining population. Loma suffered during the thirteen-hour flight; being incarcerated in a plane on such a long-haul flight with limited space was not enjoyable. She was irritated by the children making noise despite coping and loving her grandchildren. The stress of travel combined with the lack of sleep had a negative impact on her nerves. *I am too old for this.* She had aches and pains all over her body.

When the hostess came to greet the passengers, she paid special attention to Loma. It had spread by word of mouth that she was related to Emirati royalty and the treatment she received was preferential. Her economy ticket was upgraded to a business one for a pittance.

The plane's crew was made up of various nationalities from all over the globe. An eastern-European hostess approached her and asked if Loma needed some help. Loma asked her to get her hand-baggage from the compartment above her head.

The wait wasn't very long, but it seemed ages to Loma before she arrived at Pearson Airport customs. By then she was bewildered and needed help from the ground staff who were busy as they tried to do their best to help many passengers.

A young blond immigration officer glanced at her passport. The words *The Republic of Iraq* put him into a panic which was reflected in the expression on his face. He started to ask her endless questions. Who are you? How long will you stay in Canada? What is the purpose of your visit? Where will you stay? Then there were questions about her visa sponsor. Endless questions, some of them Loma could not answer let alone understand. She relived her past experiences of travelling in the old days when she held a diplomatic passport because her husband worked at the Iraqi Embassy in the United Kingdom. She was treated like minor royalty then. Alas, times had changed. She gave a sigh of relief when her passport was stamped. She collected her luggage from the carousel where she had to deal with it herself. It was not like Dubai Airport where porters did it for you or even better, back in the embassy days when embassy employees took charge of such tasks. She pushed her luggage on the trolley to the exit where she found her niece, Randa waving from behind the barrier. She had changed a great deal. She had put on weight, after having three children. Her hair was dyed blondish to match her fair skin, but Loma felt it looked artificial. Then she noticed that she'd had lip enhancement, which is not popular in the Middle East. It was a western trend.

Randa ran towards Loma and hugged her dearly. 'I have missed you Aunty, it has been a long time.'

'I know, my dear, Iraqi diaspora are scattered now because of too many wars. Our country has suffered.' Loma sighed.

Randa drove her four-by-four Nissan car from the airport car park to the Mississauga district, which was close by on the outskirts of Toronto. The suburb had flourished since it became a popular destination for immigrants, particularly those from the Middle and the Far East. Some had bought houses with the money they had brought from their native countries or after establishing themselves in their adopted country.

Loma enjoyed the fresh air and the greenery. She found it a lovely change.

'Indeed, but it is not the same in winter when the snow arrives, and temperatures drop to minus twenty.' Randa's statement did not sit well with Loma and her dreamy state of escapism. She woke up to the harsh reality of life, including the extremes of the weather.

They reached the big house that was so different to her small flat in Dubai. Randa's children looked in puzzlement at their mother's aunt when she took off her scarf and exposed her dyed brown hair. Randa led her to a bedroom with an ensuite. Loma loved it. 'I want to take you to Niagara Falls. We will show you; me and my husband. It will be soon. I am not sure when because he works long hours.'

Loma responded with a soft smile. 'I have always wanted to go there. I've seen it on films.'

Loma sat on her bed thinking about how her life had changed. She took out her mobile to check her messages and send messages to her family and her few friends to assure them of her safe arrival. She went through her messages, answered one from her son to let him know that she was safe, then she stopped at a message. It was from the detective agency she had used to investigate Selma's recent suspicious behaviour. She raised her eyebrows.

'What!' she shouted.

Her niece rushed into the room. 'Aunty, are you okay?'

'I couldn't be better,' Loma replied with a big smile.

Chapter Thirty-six

Worship Time

The weather was getting warmer and warmer by the day in Dubai. The forecast predicted 50 degrees centigrade in the middle of the day, which was the norm in August. At Oud Metha Road, close to Dubai Creek at Umm Hurair, it was very hot with humidity saturating the air and making breathing difficult for some. People had deserted the outdoor venues in the heat of lunchtime on Sunday in August, apart from a few devout Catholics heading to Saint Mary's Church to attend Sunday mass. Most of the attendees were of Asian origin and there were some Filipino nationals. The priest was a middle-aged Asian who stood at the door of the church to greet the worshippers with a smile. He tried to cope with the outdoor heat, but his heavy cassock made him feel the urgent need to get inside to refresh himself in the air-conditioned hall of the church.

Two women stood at the entrance. The younger Indian one was comforting the older one who was trying to remove her head scarf with shaking hands. She had freshly dyed black hair that hid years of wisdom and experience, which had given her grey hair. Her make-up was nicely done, but it was more for a party than for worship. She was shaking with hesitation and fear, plus the debilitating hot weather. The priest approached and greeted them according to the arrangement he had made with Rana, who was holding Selma's sweaty hand as she guided them to the main church hall.

'Welcome to bath of truth,' he said warmly to Selma. The meeting was orchestrated by Rana, after Selma disclosed her intention to convert to Christianity. Selma was given a VIP welcome by the priest. She had been deliberating over her conversion from Islam to Christianity for some time. Then she approached Rana and asked her about the process, including its consequences. Her clandestine conversion had been in progress for a while, and she had been attending

150

religious education and bible readings through social media. Selma told Rana that she'd had a premonition and to convert to Christianity for a long time. She told Rana and the priest that she'd had visions of Jesus and he had visited her in her dreams, and she felt the need to fulfil his wish for her to change. Although Selma's background was Muslim, she had never been devoutly religious, having grown up in a secular era in Iraq where people wavered between westernisation or socialism and the move away from religion then, had dominated her parents' and grandparents' culture.

After considerable thought, Selma had started to attend church with Rana. Conversion was a risky business. Islamic movements were getting stronger in the Middle East, and there had been a call to apply Islamic Sharia law to punish those who quit Islam for another religion. Selma pretended to be a practising Muslim in front of Sheikha Hasna to impress her and persuade her that she was abiding by her religion and God. Selma had kept her conversion under wraps with immense secrecy. The only person who was aware of her change was Rana, and her son, Ahmed. He was also in the process of undergoing the same change but with even more caution because of the dire consequences.

In the church hall, she sat on a solid pine bench that was hard and uncomfortable. The priest had delivered his sermon in English. Selma could not focus on the subject of caring for others. She shrugged off his topic to forget and forgive. Every now and then, Selma was comforted by Rana caressing her hands. Selma felt suffocated by the situation. Her attitude to religion would make it difficult to understand or even pretend to be genuine, but she had to follow the plan. She loathed the dominating aspect of most religions to control the masses and knew it was not for her. But she must go ahead with what she had started. The mass was so long that she lost interest and concentration. Equally, she could not focus on last Friday's Muslim prayers. They too were irrelevant to her beliefs.

At the end of the sermon, the priest greeted her warmly in broken Arabic. '*Al salamu alaykum.*' His Arabic was good enough to communicate. He reintroduced himself with more details about his background and where he came from.

'Thanks for coming. We welcome you with open arms,' he said and bowed to her out of respect.

'Thanks for having me,' but her inner voice was hissing, *Get away from me*. He started to explain the baptism procedure with its boring details, and she had to stifle her giggling.

'Please, feel free to ask anything,' he replied.

'I would be grateful to you if you could keep this matter confidential.' Selma lowered her voice and looked around to make sure that no nosy people were listening.

'Of course, Ma'am. We are aware of the sensitivity of the subject and the ramifications of your wise decision on you, and us as an institution.'

Selma left with Rana, indifferent to the other churchgoers who were willing to greet her and welcome her to the church, but she did not want to be recognised by the crowd, after having all the reassurances of confidentiality.

At the back door of the church, she hailed a taxi to Dubai Mall to meet her son for a late lunch before heading home to their flat in Sharjah. The sun was very strong, and she rushed into the air-conditioned taxi after waving goodbye to Rana.

The traffic was less busy than on working days and her journey took half the usual time. At her favourite cafe, Paul she chose her favourite hidden table. Her son arrived wearing a T-shirt and tight Jeans.

'Hello, Mother.' He kissed her on the cheek.

'Hello, darling. How was your day?'

'Fine but more importantly, how was yours?'

'Keep quiet!' She was mortified by the loudness of his voice and checked to see if anyone was nearby.

'Do they suspect what you are up to?' he asked more quietly.

'No, Rana's been helpful for me to fit in with that crowd. She trusts me and they trust her. The priest was kind despite my concerns about his honesty. But I have to put up with this nonsense called religion. You know I am not keen on Islam or any other religions.' She sipped her coffee with a jerky movement that indicated her discontent with the whole scenario.

'Look, it's a serious matter. We have applied for asylum to the United Nations on the basis of religious persecution. But we need to prove it. The church is our only hope for it to be granted. The Catholic Church in Canada has sponsored us on those grounds. We cannot risk the massive loss.' In his frustration he pushed the table and spilt coffee on the tablecloth.

'I'm not sure if I should have listened to your advice. What will happen to us if someone finds out? Even, if the Emirati Government is lenient about the matter, I'm not sure about the fundamentalists who are growing in number. I am worried.' She checked the table next to them where two Lebanese ladies sat chatting in Arabic, which made Selma even more suspicious and paranoid, in case they heard what they were talking about.

'Let's go home,' she said. It was more an order than a request.

'I thought that you wanted to do some window shopping.'

'Who gives the toss about window shopping.' She lifted her body with some difficulty as she tried to leave in haste. Her son was surprised by her fast steps, but he followed her. He wondered what was going on in his mother's mind.

Chapter Thirty-seven

Unsolved Mystery

Dubai roads were semi-deserted in the middle of the day during the summer school holidays. The usual summer exodus of the local inhabitants of the UAE was at its optimum.

At Sheikh Hasna's office it was a different story. It was very quiet since the holiday season had started. Meanwhile, the remainder of the staff were skiving off an hour or two before the end of the day in the absence of management.

Hasna made it a priority to reconnect with her grandchildren, particularly the youngest one who is still suffering from physical and mental health problems. Her times in the office were few and far between.

In the meantime, Selma was finding every and any excuse to leave early or arrive late. Her main excuse was that she was suffering physical health problems after her confrontation with Loma. In reality, she was spending the majority of her absence between the church, the United Nations centre for refugees and the Canadian Embassy. She had to attend interviews, which were time consuming, and she had to sort out the paperwork associated with her refugee application and also make travel preparations.

Loma entered the office suffering from a headache and jet lag after the long direct journey from Toronto to Dubai. She asked the porter to get her a strong Arabic coffee from the coffee kiosk down the road. Then she asked the secretary if Selma was in her office. The secretary wanted to pour out all her suffering about Selma's rude and aggressive manners and behaviour. She had picked up on the acrimonious state between the two rivals.

'She is not rude to everyone, though,' she said.

Loma had enough information to denounce Selma before Hasna and others. She did not need further proof or evidence against her

154

enemy. She tried to discontinue the conversation with the secretary so as not to escalate the situation further, and avoid more confrontations, as she had promised her boss. She asked the secretary to leave with polite apologetic words. 'Not to worry, we will sort it out soon, very soon.'

Not long after, there was a knock on her office door. The secretary entered in a hurry.

'Madam, there is a gentleman who wants to see you, but he declined to give his name.'

'How strange. That is not usual. He should identify himself,' Loma replied with anxiety.

'I tried, but he was adamant he had to talk to you in private. He said it was confidential.'

'Okay, let him in.'

A man in his forties who spoke Arabic with a Palestinian accent came in. He was tall with a slim figure except for his protruding stomach. As-salamu alaykum,' he greeted Loma.

Loma reciprocated and asked him to sit down.

'I am a private detective. My name is Bader. I'm sorry, I could not disclose my identity to your staff.'

'Welcome. I think we have corresponded by email and phone, but we have never met.' Loma felt reassured by his presence.

'Exactly, Ma'am. According to our previous discussion, I have the proof about the woman you suspect of religion conversion.' He opened his briefcase and took out photos that showed Selma in the church undergoing the rite of Christian initiation, step by step.

Loma opened her mouth with surprise. She was aware of Selma's aversion to any religion, and she had never been a practising Muslim. She thought that there must be something behind such a drastic change. She wondered what Selma was up to. She pulled herself from her thoughts. She had to collect more facts. 'Do you have more documentation to confirm this?' Loma asked with a smile as she looked through the photos. She took particular interest in the ones where Selma was kissing the hand of the priest.

'No, Ma'am, nothing apart from the photos. It is confidential and particularly in her case there is extra security to maintain the confidentiality. No one would have access to such documents even the intelligence would not.'

'Not to worry. I have enough evidence. Seemingly, she is attending church regularly, in the open.' She took a deep breath then paused before she spoke again. 'I will transfer the balance of your fees to your agency's bank account.' Loma waved with her hand to terminate the meeting.

'Thanks, Ma'am.' He stood up, bowed to her, pleased with his customers' high satisfaction rating, and left.

Loma giggled. *Who is it who laughs last?* She picked up her mobile and touched the screen to reveal the messages. She dialled a number and heard the click as the answering machine picked up the call. 'Hello, this is Selma, I am busy right now; please leave a message and I will get back to you soon.'

Loma touched the digits that would allow her to leave a message on the answering machine. 'Hi dear. It's Loma. I'm back from Canada. I came to the office to see you. I miss you, dear. Can we catch up as soon as possible? But not in the office.' She ended the call triumphant. 'It is my turn now,' she said in a loud voice.

Chapter Thirty-eight

Do Peaks Meet?

The Japanese car powered along the busy motorway separating the principality of Dubai from the one in Sharjah. The road was very busy with vehicles expelling exhaust fumes from air-conditioned cars. The pollution made it difficult to breathe outside the car. The driver stopped at a tall building called The Tower in the industrial area of Sharjah to check the address given to him by Loma who was sitting in the rear seat.

She had covered her hair with a black veil, and she wore large-framed Chanel sunglasses in an attempt to hide her face. Loma did not want to be seen or recognised. She was aware of a significant number of Iraqi ex-pats who resided in Sharjah, where the rent was cheaper in comparison to Dubai. Her visit needed to be a secret at any price. The Asian driver opened the door to talk to Loma from a distance to check that the address was correct. Loma pulled her tiny slim figure upright. She wore a pistachio green jacket and loose trousers of the same colour. Her Ecco shoes were to stop her chronic backache from getting worse. She had recently suffered an injury to her spine.

The chauffeur opened the main door of building number twelve and pressed the lift buttons. Loma thanked him and entered the lift alone. She felt that the driver knew more than she wanted, but she could not help that. Her fingers were wet with sweat caused by anxiety, and they made sticky fingerprints on her mobile screen. Loma walked slowly making a noise with her shoes on the smooth Italian marble floor. She had felt suffocated in the lift, as if she were in a closet. She could hardly remember the number of the floor or the flat's number. The lift door opened into a dim corridor that smelt of detergent and reminded her of the smell in a hospital. Was the number of the flat seven or eight? She chose the latter. She rang the doorbell, but there was no response. Then she tried number seven. After several attempts at ringing and knocking and not receiving a response, she decided to leave, but suddenly, the door opened. Selma appeared wearing a loose gown and looking unkempt with no make-up.

'Loma, what are you doing here?' she cried.

'I was worried about you; you disappeared without leaving contact details. Are you going to let me in?' Loma's tone held the upper hand.

'Certainly, sorry I'm not how I'm supposed to be. You should have called; it's normal under the circumstances.' Selma's voice was full of disdain.

'It's urgent, and I didn't want to talk to you at the office or in a public place. I left several messages on your answering machine without realising that you were not living in Dubai anymore and you hadn't informed work or given a reason for your absence from work.' Loma sat down without permission and Selma opened her mouth wide with surprise.

'Really, what is so urgent?' Selma picked up a packet of cigarettes from the table without offering Loma one, lit one and puffed the smoke in Loma's direction. Loma fanned the fumes with her hands.

'Well, I'll be upfront with you. I've learnt that you have changed your religion.'

The statement shocked Selma. She threw her cigarette on the floor and extinguished it with her shoe. 'Nonsense. You're a pathological liar. Get out of my house!' Selma stood upright. Her tall figure was enhanced by her loud voice.

Loma opened her handbag, took out the photos and handed them to Selma. She snatched them out of Loma's hand and stared at them. 'This has nothing to do with me.'

'It's you and it has been confirmed by Rana who has signed a confession.' She showed her a copy of the signed statement. 'There is no point in denying it. You've been caught red-handed. You know the ramifications of conversion. You will be lucky to escape Sharia law, or the fundamentalist groups but not Hasna's disrespect or the Muslim community in general.'

'I will deny everything and complain to the human rights' organisations.' Her reply resonated with fear and anxiety.

'Well, let's hear your word against mine. The church will denounce you when they learn that you are a fraud and a big liar, and there is no way that you can justify what you have done in front of everyone. You are a loser either way.'

Selma held herself together to stop her body from shaking, but still she trembled, and tears poured from her eyes and mixed with her black kohl eyeliner, the only make-up she was wearing. Her tone had changed from the one in control and to the one begging, much to Loma's astonishment. She hadn't expected such a change of tactic from the usually strong domineering woman. Selma fell heavily onto the arm of the sofa.

'You cannot imagine how much we've suffered to get to where we are now. You knew we had become skint. My husband fritted away his father's fortune on drinks and prostitutes. I only have my son; my daughter is locked in a miserable marriage. And work is getting scarce in this country. My son is out of work or about to be. He was dismissed unfairly, so we planned to emigrate to Canada. The only way to get our application approved was to get the church's sponsorship and we had to convert. But I will never change. I resisted the Islamic fundamentalist movement back home after the fall of the State, and I am faithful to my beliefs and principles, not others,' Selma fell into the old sofa.

Loma stared at her. 'Is this you, the mighty, stern, feisty woman who scared half of Baghdad society with her vicious attitude, sharp tongue and gossip. What an irony; Selma is weak and begging for mercy now, and from who? Me!'

'Please, do not ruin all that I have planned for a long time.' Her begging confused Loma.

'You have already ruined my life by depriving me of the only love of my life and you did not stop at that. You continued to threaten me with exposing my secret that I had lost my virginity to a cowardly man, your brother-in-law, my old flame as he continues to be. Not only losing the love of my life, but I lost his baby too. You wanted to destroy my reputation by exposing me to Hasna and others. Is there any other reason for having a feud?'

Loma headed to the door while Selma slipped from the armchair to the floor, weeping and begging.

Loma turned as she stood at the door. 'I feel sorry for you, but you deserve no mercy.' She shut the door with force.

Selma wiped her crocodile tears and rushed to her mobile and dialled a number she knew by heart. When her son answered she started shouting. 'Disaster! Hurry and come back home. I cannot talk to you on the phone.'

'Mother, what is wrong?'

'Just come and I will tell you.' She ended the call with shaking hands and called the maid. 'You can have a break for the day. Just leave now.'

The maid who understood Arabic was surprised her employer was so mean and offered her holidays and short breaks.

Ahmed rushed out of his office and hailed a taxi in front of the building. He left his car behind in the company car park.

When Selma heard a noise at her door, she became terrified that someone was trying to get in. Then the door opened and there was Ahmed with sweat droplets on his forehead.

'Mother, what is the problem?'

Selma asked him to check if the maid had left the flat and ushered him closer. 'Loma is aware of everything.'

'What do you mean?'

'She knows about our conversion and the rest of it. She is threatening to tell Hasna and the authorities.'

'Disaster! It will be the end of us.'

'We need to act promptly.'

'How?' His muddled thinking prevented him from planning any action.

Selma banged the coffee table with her fist. 'We need to have an urgent and safe exit from here. We cannot afford any deviation from our plan. I'm worried that they apply Sharia law on us, but I am even more worried that we could be picked up by an extremist group. Then that would be the end.' She looked for a cigarette.

Her son knew that she was angry and irritable when she asked for a smoke.

She turned swiftly. 'Do we have any alcohol at home?'

'I bought a bottle of red wine from the shop the other day.'

'Go and get us two glasses. I need to focus on plan B.' She puffed her cigarette from a smirking mouth.

'What plan, Mother?'

'We are living in a dangerous world with a changeable climate. We need to adapt. And, in order to adapt, we need air-conditioning to adjust to the change of the weather.'

'Mother, be careful, remember what has happened to Malaka and Zelfa.' He poured the wine into the glasses with fear radiating from his hazel eyes.

'It's a jungle, my dear, and we are the animals. We need to comply with the jungle rules. It's a matter of being strong enough to eat because the weak get eaten. Escape is the advice for the latter to survive.' She slugged back her glass of wine and asked for more. When the alcohol entered her bloodstream, she knew she would become calmer.

Chapter Thirty-nine

About to Say Farewell

The microphone was filling the air with announcements at Dubai Airport. The airport crowd was jabbering like parrots — different languages and different nationalities from all over the globe.

Selma entered the airport wearing tight pink trousers and a black shirt. She was bare-headed, having removed her *hejab* in haste as soon as she left the taxi. Perhaps she should have kept it on because she was concerned about other passengers' curious looks and she was paranoid about her sudden change of appearance. Yet she felt the freedom that she longed for, for the first time ever.

Her son followed her and pushed the trolley with three large suitcases. She pretended that she was in charge, and that she knew everything despite her limited English vocabulary. Ahmed checked-in their luggage with Emirates Airlines for the flight heading directly to Toronto. He was in such a state that he became breathless. He could hardly string together one sentence, but managed to after he took a deep breath.

'I have checked in the luggage and here is your boarding pass, Mother. They checked the visa and there was no problem.'

'Thank goodness for that. The recent unrest caused by that bitch Loma helped us in the end. We were granted asylum for religious persecution.' She grinned much to her son's surprise. She had yelled and howled after Loma threatened to expose her to society and the authorities.

'Mother, she did a good deed by not reporting your conversion from Islam. You would not want the consequences.'

'Listen, son, there is no free lunch. She did what she did because I would have exposed her secret, the one that will follow her to her grave. To announce such a secret to the public, and particularly Hasna would be the end of her. Do not forget she is affiliated with the previous

162

regime which is unpopular among many Iraqis and others. Her arrogance would not allow her to appreciate how kind I was to her.'

'Well, she could be granted political asylum, if she applied,' he said as he looked at a sea of passengers who were trying to catch their flights on time.

'That's another story. She is carrying a lot of baggage, especially her story about the disappearance of her husband or ex-husband, if I may say so. Westerners would consider her an enemy because of her affiliation with Saddam's regime. She deserves all the harm in the world.'

The pair could not wait any longer and wanted to get through customs as soon as possible. They had had sleepless nights since the dreadful meeting between Selma and Loma and Loma and her son's relentless efforts to prepare a prompt exit plan to leave the country. They approached the United Nations High Commission for Refugees (UNHCR) and pleaded to be removed to a different country. They were not allowed to travel to their native Iraq and despite UAE being deemed a safe country, if they remained there, they risked being punished by Islamic laws for conversion. Nevertheless, the UNHCR process would take time and Selma was told that their application could be rejected. It was a lengthy process, and it could take years for a decision on their applications. They were living a nightmare every day and worried about being targeted by extremists or being deported. And then there was the community perception that they had pretended they were converts to achieve their goal to emigrate to the West. Travel was a problem because they did not have United Nations passports. But Ahmed had met a shady character who had forged two false Canadian passports to enable them to travel to Canada and apply for asylum there.

Selma woke up from her absent-minded state at the sound of Ahmed's loud voice.

'Come on, Mother, I have checked in the luggage; let's go to immigration.

Selma tried to run, but it was difficult given her age and her limited movement. Or perhaps she was frozen out of fear.

They approached the immigration booth. Selma examined the immigration officers in the hope of analysing their psyche. She could not read much apart from their tough facial expressions that indicated their professionalism. She saw young men wearing traditional clothing, a white *dishdasha* and ekal head covering. The female officers were wearing headscarves and heavy make-up. Her intuition led her to a middle-aged woman with average good looks. She hoped she had low self-esteem, and she recalled her belief that ugly women have low self-esteem.

'Let's go to booth number three,' she said to her son. He followed her like a sheep to green grass.

'*Al salamu alaykum.*' They uttered their greetings in unison. Her voice came across strong and confident while anxiety got the better of Ahmed, and his voice was weak and hesitant.

The officer responded with a bow. Ahmed handed over the two passports and the boarding passes with hesitation. Selma was shaking as she tried to keep the woman busy. Ahmed answered questions about his job and why they were leaving the country. His anxiety tied his tongue even more. Selma stepped in to take over, but the officer realised there was a problem. She opened the passport and looked at Selma and Ahmed. 'Are you United Nations refugees?'

Selma pushed Ahmed. 'Yes, we are, and we've been accepted in Canada,' he said.

The woman pulled a face that showed discontent. She picked up the telephone, dialled a number and began whispering in a deliberate attempt to conceal the content of her conversation from the terrified couple. They looked at each other in despair and the seconds seemed like minutes to them. Then, a short young local man, wearing a khaki military suit, arrived. He saluted politely and asked them to follow him. Selma's legs struggled to hold her upright and she felt the urge to pee. The young man guided them to a small room without a window. Loma sat on the sofa and felt suffocated as she relived her prison experience in Iraq many years ago. She suffered flashbacks of her torture, which resulted in her weeping loudly. Her son imitated her and made an even louder noise. A middle-aged Emirati man, wearing traditional dress, opened the door and tried to calm her down with soothing, comforting words, but they had no effect on her. Then he turned to Ahmed and asked him to man up in a harsh tone and support his mother. The younger man came across and pulled Ahmed from the sofa. 'He is innocent. He did not do anything,' Selma shouted.

'Lady, you are using fake travel papers,' the older man said. The younger security man pushed Ahmed out of the room to the sound of his mother's wailing. The older man turned to her. 'You are not free to go; we will be interrogating both of you.'

'I did not know where to go. We gave up our flat with all our furniture and we have no money left.' The older man simply stared at her. 'I would rather to be in prison with my son,' she added.

First, they searched her handbag and checked her mobile. When they gave it back, Selma wanted to throw it away, but when the older man left the room temporarily she pressed the icon with the name LOMA and left a message.

'I am in trouble. I need your help.'

Chapter Forty

Unexpected Reaction

The four-by-four Toyota car snaked along the well-paved road in the desert outside the hustle and bustle of Dubai. The road signs indicated it was heading to the Al Awir Deportation Jail. The driver knew the way well, having been there many times to escort the nearest and dearest of imprisoned women, whereas his passenger was in shock and disbelief about the trip.

Loma was going to visit someone who had been in prison before. She was reliving the memory when she visited Selma at Abu Ghraib Prison in Baghdad over twenty years ago. It seemed that history kept repeating itself; she was on her way to visit Selma in prison again. She had experienced only a small guilt trip; she did not have a direct hand in causing her imprisonment. After Selma and her son had been detained for forging travel documents at Dubai Airport, Selma had been calling Loma asking for help.

Selma still wondered if Loma had been responsible for her, and her son being imprisoned in different prisons in a foreign country without any indication of when they would be released.

Loma thought about Selma and her plight with some sympathy. Hence, she had obtained a permit to visit Selma.

The receptionist at the prison was an obese local woman whose hair was covered with a flowery scarf. Her heavy make-up was in competition with the colourful scarf. The woman read the note handed to her by the driver while Loma watched from a distance through her dark Chanel sunglasses. The receptionist stood up and greeted Loma who came forward. She was wearing a dark jacket and a long skirt. She opened the main gate and ushered Loma in. A different younger woman led her to a big hall with wooden benches. Visitors were flocking in, followed by female prisoners who rushed forward to get moral support from those who continued to care about them. Most of the women were Asian, African or Arab nationalities. They were serving sentences for illegal prostitution, drug smuggling and other crimes ranging from petty crime to murder. Many were there because they'd stayed longer than their residence permit allowed. Loma sat on the bench staring at the crowd as she looked for Selma. She sensed for the first time that even though they had a love-hate relationship, sometimes they complemented each other.

Loma was in emotional turmoil, when she heard a familiar voice, although it was not as fierce as it used to be — it was weak and broken. She glanced at Selma who seemed to have become older and thinner during the weeks of her imprisonment. Her hair was covered with an orange scarf that matched her voluminous gown. Her wrinkles had increased and there were bags under her eyes. Loma stood up and was greeted by an unexpected strong hug from Selma.

'Thank you for responding to my message to visit me,' Selma said.

'Not at all. I hope you are well,' Loma replied in a quiet voice.

'I'm worried about my son. I haven't heard from him since we were detained at the airport,' Selma said.

'Don't worry, I asked Hamid our office manager to pay him a visit and he is okay.'

'Thank you. You have done me a great favour that I will not forget it.' Selma's voice was full of gratitude. Loma couldn't tell if it was genuine or false.

'It was nothing, but we need to clarify what is going on between us. The hate and vengeance need to come to an end.' Loma really wanted to settle the matter with Selma.

'I have nothing against you. Do not forget you took the drastic measure of putting me in prison in Iraq, if you remember. I hope you did not have a hand in this.' Selma's voice became stronger as she regained her sense of power.

Loma pulled a horror-stricken face and stood up abruptly. 'How could you accuse me of that?'

'You have a history, my dear, and proven history, but I forgive you. Please help me.' Selma lowered her tone as she begged for rescue, and equally wanted to make Loma feel guilty. Selma's reaction revived Loma's feelings of repulsion towards her. Her past was like a movie trailer. She had been separated from the love of her life and suffered as a result because of Selma. And she remembered how vindictive Selma had been, but had she changed? She came back from her journey into the past to hear Selma's plea for help.

'Not to worry, I have been in touch with a lawyer who has contacted the United Nations office. He thinks that the recent events will consolidate your claim for asylum in the West as the United Arab Emirates is categorized as an unsafe place,' Loma spoke quickly. Then she left abruptly much to Selma's surprise and ongoing plea to rescue her, as she asked God to protect her and her family. Loma did not want the conversation to deteriorate as they always had in the past.

Loma rushed to the main gate where the female guard opened the door using a key from the enormous bunch clipped to her belt.

As she searched for the driver who was waiting in the car park, she thought about Selma. *She will never change.* She could not hide her glee at Selma's misfortune.

On the other side of the fence, in the prison, Selma was staring at the horizon and also thinking. *Would Loma help her? She was a bitch.* She came back to the present when she heard harsh, loud shouting of the woman jailer in charge. 'Visiting is finished. Leave the hall immediately.'

The prisoners protested about the short amount of time they were allowed to see their loved ones. It was never long enough — never.

Selma sighed loudly. Was it a relief that she had shared her burden? She had come to realise that her fate was in Loma's hands. She would rather die than submit to her, but she must continue to play the game to the end. Her survival instinct would prevail. She remembered the words of her English teacher; *Survival is for the fittest.* She bit her lip as she tried to resist the jailer's hands pushing her shoulder to make her leave.

Chapter Forty-one

Judgement

Loma sat in the office holding a cup of strong Arabic coffee. She tried to sip slowly, but she was eager to get a high level of caffeine into her system. She was dependent on caffeine. And she noticed the difference in her mood and focus after the first few sips. She was dreading coping without coffee when she had to observe Ramadan which was coming soon. After a loud knock on her office door, the Asian porter entered without waiting as he used to. Loma showed her anger by glaring at him, but he was indifferent and hellbent on delivering his urgent message. 'Sheikha Hasna is in the office, and she wants to see now,' he said.

Loma gave up her speech to teach him manners and office etiquette. He left the door ajar, and Loma rushed to look at her face in the mirror to ensure her scarf was well-adjusted. Luckily, she had not put on too much make-up. She hurried along the corridor ignoring the employees' astonished looks as she marched past. She knocked on Hasna's office door and heard a sharp, loud irritated reply. 'Come in.'

Hasna was wearing a long gown without a matching head scarf, contrary to her habit of being colour-coordinated with her outfits and accessories. She told Loma to sit with a movement of her hand. Loma's attention was distracted by the brilliance of the diamonds on Hasna's Cartier watch. Her manner was aloof, and lacked her usual warmth which gave Loma cause for concern. She started the conversation in a very official tone.

'I'm not happy with the latest news.' Hasna avoided direct eye contact with Loma to keep her serious facade.

'What has happened? Have I done something?' Loma's voice was shaky and so too were her hands in keeping with her elevated level of anxiety because her boss was angry with her.

'It is Selma; I understand that she is prison. Why did you keep it a secret from me? And, you have been to visit her in prison, and you never mentioned a word.' Hasna banged her fist on the leather desktop.

'I never meant to undermine you or belittle you. I just didn't want to disturb you with such a minute thing; I know how busy you have been with your grandson's recent health scare.'

'Selma has been in contact with me. She told me that she is in prison because you slandered her. I understand you have a long history of disagreement, feud and huge differences but to cause such harm to her; it is unacceptable and unfair.'

Loma felt the heat coming from her toes and rising upwards. She was mortified at the thought that Selma might have revealed her secret — a secret that she had spent the majority of her life hiding from everyone, including Hasna.

'I had nothing to do with it. I paid her a visit in prison to make sure she was well.'

'I've heard a different story, that you accused her blasphemy and she had to flee the country.'

'That is not true. You would have been informed in due course. You are the boss here.'

'I have been in touch with a relative who works at Dubai Airport Intelligence. He confirmed that she was using fake travel documents. It is a serious offence and Emirati authorities may deport her. The problem is that Selma and her son hold Iraqi passports and they could be sent to Baghdad.' Hasna's tone was full of genuine concern.

'Oh dear, it is serious. It is not safe to go back now. Not, when you have been deported for forging travel documents.' Loma felt guilty. Yes, she'd had a hand in what had happened. It was her revenge. Her feud with Selma was eternal. She was hoping that Hasna would never find out the truth.

'However, I hope it will not take place. I have learnt that the United Nations has intervened. I did not realise Selma and her son had applied for asylum. They have been granted it obviously after all those events. I hope they can travel to a safer destination,' Hasna said.

Loma was shocked by this revelation. She could not balance her anger with her relief. Her main goal was that Selma would not disclose her secret to Hasna and others.

'Please, try to get a lawyer to help her.' Hasna issued an order.

'May I say something?' Loma's voice was quiet for fear of her boss's reaction.

'What?' Hasna was looking at a pile of papers on her desk.

'I just wanted to highlight that Selma has dodgy connections and I am worried about your reputation.'

Loma's statement came as a surprise to Hasna. Before Hasna could respond Loma continued. 'Maybe better you distance yourself from her. I will make sure that the United Nations are aware of the situation and that they take charge of the case.'

Hasna looked up to the ceiling as she gave Loma's suggestion consideration. 'Okay, I will leave it to you.'

'Excellent, please leave all the communication with Selma to me too.' Loma left the room with a huge sigh of relief, thankful that her secret was still a secret, for now at least. She had won the first round.

Chapter Forty-two

Goodbye or au Revoir

Dubai airport was busy with passengers because it was the holiday season. Tourists or sun worshippers were heading to this part of the world with the hope of boosting their vitamin D levels from the golden rays.

A group of the local police personnel marched through the departure gates. Selma was in the middle of the group. She was looking up to where the immigration officers were based and hoping to see her son. She was wearing a long black gown with a matching headscarf. A young man from airport security was kind to carry her small suitcase that contained her basic needs. The scene attracted the curiosity of the passengers intrigued about why a middle-aged woman had been detained by the police. Selma was talking loudly to attract the attention of the other passengers.

'I refuse to board the plane without my son,' she shouted to the police.

'Madam, he will follow us soon,' the young policeman replied in a polite tone.

The loudspeakers deafened Selma's ears with an announcement about the Canadian Airlines flight to Toronto.

Since she had been in prison and the United Nations had recognised her and her asylum application, she had been granted refugee status with a permit to live in Canada. It had been her dream to emigrate but never alone.

While Selma was ranting about not leaving without her son, Loma appeared. Selma stopped shouting and looked at her.

'Well, well. Look who's here, Miss Innocent. Aren't I the honoured one to receive a visit from you?'

'I wanted to say goodbye.'

'How dare you to patronise me. You orchestrated the whole thing.' Selma tried to advance and hit Loma with her handbag, but the young policeman was too quick for her. He held Selma and restrained her while Loma tottered on her high-heeled designer shoes as she tried to escape Selma's assault.

'I had nothing to do with it. I have mediated for you so you could get a peaceful and dignified exit out of all the mess that *you* have created.' Loma advanced slowly towards Selma, who had become calmer. 'I am here to settle things between us,' Loma added.

'There is nothing but bad blood between us,' Selma spat.

'Yes, I want to apologise. I had you imprisoned in Iraq and Emirates too. You cannot imagine the fear and insecurity I endure every time I hear your name, let alone having to be close to you in the office. What were you hoping to gain? Tell me.' Loma's voice became loud so she could be heard over the airport loudspeakers.

Selma struggled free from the tight hold of the policeman and advanced carefully towards Loma, defying the policeman who tried to stop her. 'You must understand, we will never like each other, and this will continue until the judgment day.'

'Why do you hate me?' Loma asked.

'I have always detested you. You got everything I could not have. The man I loved. Yes, I loved my brother-in-law and I tried to get his heart, but you snatched him from me. You deprived me of everything I loved in life. You are always the winner, and I am second-rate.' Selma's confession showed how fragile and vulnerable she was, contrary to the stiff and rigid facade she always put on.

Loma pitied her. She was the monster she had feared all her life. Selma was the genie in the lamp, waiting to unleash her destructive power. But now she seemed weak and fragile. *Was I fighting an illusion?*

Selma came closer to Loma even though she feared her unpredictable behaviour. 'I want to leave but with my son. I am nothing without him.'

'You did not give me the chance to deliver my message. I have obtained a pardon for you and your son. He will join you soon. Hasna paid a lawyer to take your case with the United Nations to gain asylum status and you were successful.'

'I wish I could believe you.' Selma look was like an arrow piercing Loma's heart.

'Believe me for once. We will never get on well, but can we tolerate each other.' Her words were interrupted by Ahmed, who was handcuffed, and shouting. The minute he spotted his mother, he started to cry. Then he turned his head and saw Loma.

'You again! Go to hell!'

Selma raised her voice. 'Stop it, son. Leave her alone. Let's leave without noise.' She turned to Loma.

'Thanks for nothing. I will never forgive you for what you did to me. Who knows when we will meet again.' At that moment the police led Selma and her son towards customs.

Loma walked outside the airport where the loudspeaker announcements faded gradually.

'Canadian Airlines flight to Toronto; gates are now closed.'

THE END

Milton Keynes UK
Ingram Content Group UK Ltd.
UKHW052052300624
444882UK00001B/65